HOURS BEFORE DARK

Jo Hammond

ORCA BOOK PUBLISHERS

Copyright © 2005 Jo Hammond

All rights reserved. No part of this publication may be reproduced
or transmitted in any form or by any means, electronic or mechanical, including
photocopying, recording or by any information storage and retrieval system now known
or to be invented, without permission in writing from the publisher.

National Library of Canada Cataloguing in Publication Data

Hammond, Jo, 1941-
Home before dark / Jo Hammond.

ISBN 1-55143-340-0

I. Title.

PS8615.A544H65 2005   jC813'.6   C2005-902052-0

Summary: Erik and his friends stumble across a decades-old crime in the coastal rainforest.

First published in the United States, 2005

Library of Congress Control Number: 2005924731

Orca Book Publishers gratefully acknowledges the support for its publishing programs
provided by the following agencies: the Government of Canada through the Book
Publishing Industry Development Program (BPIDP), the Canada Council for the Arts,
and the British Columbia Arts Council.

Cover design: Lynn O'Rourke
Cover artwork: Karel Doruyter

Orca Book Publishers   Orca Book Publishers
Box 5626, Stn. B   PO Box 468
Victoria, BC   Canada   Custer, WA USA
V8R 6S4   98240-0468

Printed and bound in Canada
08 07 06 05 • 5 4 3 2 1

To Erik

Acknowledgements
I would like to thank my mentor, Betty Keller, for her
advice; my husband, Dick, for inspiring me with his
own *Tales from Hidden Basin;* and Howard White,
for his encouragement.

TABLE OF CONTENTS

BAILOUT

ERIK Johnson hot-melted the raccoon skull onto the hood of his 1980 Subaru wagon and stood back to admire it. As he was congratulating himself on the skull's placement, his mother called from the back door, "Erik, Mike's on the phone!"

He ran into the basement and picked up the extension. "Mike?"

"Erik!" Mike shouted. "Guess what? The boat's here. Coming over?"

"See you in five," Erik answered. After telling his mother where he was going, he ran outside and jumped into his car, but not before checking that the skull was firmly stuck. He made sure his father didn't see him take off because he was afraid he'd be asked to help with an unpleasant engine-dismantling job. Erik's parents were log salvors, and their nineteen-foot aluminum-hulled work-boat, the *Snark*, had been acting up that morning. Something terminal, Mr. Johnson had suspected, like a leaking head gasket.

As Erik drove up the driveway, he made a mental note to grab the next couple of dead rats from his cats and bury them in an ant's nest; a rat skull above each headlight would look even better.

Erik lived on the waterfront and he knew about boats. He'd first driven his parents' workboat—powered by a 460 Ford coupled to a three-stage Hamilton jet—at the age of five. His own boat, which used to belong to his father, was only ten feet long, made from thick fiberglass on wood, but its broad, fairly flat hull and the twenty-horsepower Mercury outboard engine made it fly like a bird. When his dad had given it to him just after his tenth birthday, he'd painted it a deep azure blue and named it *DC-3*, after the most dependable plane ever built.

When he reached Mike Makinen's yard, about the same time as Big Dave, he was rather put out that no one noticed his new hood ornament. However, his disappointment soon vanished as he wandered around the white boat with his two friends, both, like him, in grade twelve.

Mike's almost pure white hair made him stand out in a crowd. His eyes were a startling luminous pale blue, the color often associated with champion marksmen; he participated at shooting competitions across Canada, usually coming away with a couple of trophies from each one. Before his grandmother returned to Germany at the end of the summer, she'd given Mike enough money to buy a secondhand runabout. On his father's advice, he'd waited until the beginning of October to buy it because boats were cheaper at that time of the year. As a result, he'd been able to buy a bigger and better boat than he'd hoped for.

He slapped its side. "It's a sixteen-footer."

"Hmm. A fifty-horse Merc," said Erik. "Should zip along with that."

"Does it work?" asked Dave.

"Of course," exclaimed Mike indignantly. "Dad tried it out already."

"In the water?" asked Erik.

"Didn't need to. He ran the motor in a barrel of water," Mike explained as he climbed onto the trailer's wheel. He walked along the narrow gunwale and jumped inside. "Besides, it was overhauled in the spring."

Erik had never seen Mike so excited; he was usually the quiet type—unless someone or something had annoyed him.

Big Dave joined them in the boat. He was at least an inch taller than his two friends, who were already around the six-foot mark, and his biceps were just beginning to show results from his new hobby—weight lifting. "When are you taking it out?" he asked.

"Now. When Dad's ready."

"Awesome," he said. "If you want anything painted on it, I'll do it. For free." Art was another hobby of Dave's. His uncle had recently taught him how to airbrush. He vaulted out and walked round to the bow. "It doesn't have a name. You've got to give it a name."

"I'll think of something…later," said Mike.

ERIK PHONED HOME just before they left. "Dad, is it okay if I try out Mike's new boat with him and Dave?"

"Where are you going?" asked Mr. Johnson.

"Bowen Island—Snug Cove."

"Don't you think that's a bit far for a first trip? It's blowing a strong southwesterly. Could get a bit sloppy out there."

"I know," Erik answered, "but it's sheltered most of the way."

"I'd rather you stayed home to give me a hand with my engine, but I guess I can wait another day," said Mr. Johnson. "Stay close to the shore and make sure you're home before dark. Days are shorter now that it's fall."

Erik usually paid attention to his father's warnings. Mr. Johnson had learned the hard way, and his narrow escapes out on the water made for some interesting suppertime stories.

Within an hour, all parents had been consulted and permission granted. Lifejackets and rain gear were stowed aboard ready for Mike's father to trailer the boat to the Gibsons harbor ramp.

MIKE, ERIK AND DAVE grinned with anticipation as Mike's dad backed the truck, boat and trailer down the ramp into the water. They held their breath as Mike started the outboard and marveled that it turned over on the first try.

Mike beamed. "Told you it was okay," he said.

"You be back here by 4:30," said Mr. Makinen in his soft drawling Finnish accent. He pulled the empty trailer up the ramp, parked in the lot and watched the speedboat head toward the north end of Keats Island.

THE BOAT BOUNCED ALONG on the grayish green choppy waves. The boys laughed as the wind blew the refreshing cold spray against their faces. More than a month had gone by since the beginning of September when they'd had their last swim of the year, seeing who could stay in the longest, all of them calling it quits at the same time.

Erik glanced up at the low gray clouds racing along from the southwest beneath the pale, slow-moving layer above. While the air felt cool against his skin, he pretended it was a summer afternoon, because summer meant he could forget school for a while. That was one of the reasons he liked boating. It was an escape from being cooped up in a classroom, where he had to work hard, writing about things he wasn't interested in. He took a couple of deep breaths through his nose and tried to fix the smell in his memory so that he could draw on it when he was in school. It isn't salty, he thought. And not fishy either. It's just fresh, almost a seaweedy smell.

To the right side of the boat—starboard—was Keats Island, no more than three miles long, mostly forested with dense evergreens growing amongst gray, lichen-covered granite bluffs. The two hills on the middle of the island rose to about seven hundred feet. Just above the rocky shores, most of the summer houses and cabins were empty and nearly all of their floats and ramps had already been taken out, stored in the nearest bay for the winter. A few miles across the sound, to their port side, Erik could see the much larger island of Gambier.

Once they'd cleared Keats, the wind began to hit them, but the Pasley group of islands a couple of miles to the west prevented any major swell build-up. Erik knew that they'd soon have the added protection of Bowen Island, about six times as big and three times as high as Keats.

The three of them stood shouting and grabbing onto the windshield or each other when a larger wave caused the boat to lift a bit higher and bang down unevenly. They laughed when Dave's baseball cap was blown overboard. Mike turned the wheel sharply to retrieve it, grinning wickedly as his passengers almost fell over from the force of his sudden maneuver. Dave wrung the sodden cap out and threw it under the bow. The ride to Snug Cove was far from comfortable, but they didn't mind. Within forty minutes of leaving Gibsons, they turned the corner into the sheltered cove on Bowen's east side and tied up to the government dock.

"Let's look around," suggested Dave. "We've gotta check it out now we're here."

"Okay, but not for too long," said Mike. Erik knew that Mike was nervous about leaving his new boat unguarded for even a few minutes.

They made sure that the mooring ropes had been securely tied to the dock before climbing the ramp to the road. At a store a few hundred feet further on they bought some pop and a couple of bags of chips. On their way back to the boat, they felt the first drops of rain on their faces.

Mike looked at his watch. "C'mon," he said. "It's half past three."

As they bounced down the ramp, Dave suddenly shouted, "Look! There's someone in your boat!"

A hooded man dressed in a dirty camouflage jacket was undoing one of the tie-up ropes.

"Hey! That's my boat!" Mike yelled to him.

The man turned and eyed them furtively before grabbing his backpack and jumping onto the dock. "Wrong boat," he grunted. "My friend told me to meet him here."

Mike held his breath as the smelly character strode past them. Erik pinched his nose and Dave pretended to choke. They watched him climb the ramp and walk up to the road. Finally Mike spoke. "I don't believe him."

"Sleaze bag," said Dave.

"I'll bet he was going to steal it," said Erik. The others agreed. "Besides, why did he go up to the road instead of looking for his friend down here?"

"Phew! He sure stinks!" Mike exclaimed. "Must've been sleeping rough."

"Nah," said Erik. "Too old for that."

Mike untied the bowline. "How could you tell?" he retorted. "He was hiding his face."

"I got a quick look," Erik insisted. "He's old."

"Older than your dad?" Dave asked Erik, whose father had recently turned sixty.

"Way older," said Erik.

"I wonder why he's wearing camouflage?" muttered Dave.

"It's cheap. Probably army surplus," said Erik. "My sister bought a jacket like that for five bucks."

Once they cleared Snug Cove they forgot about the stranger. Keeping close to the south arm of the bay, they followed the rocky point, further away from Gibsons.

"Weather's not so bad," said Mike. "Why don't we go back along this shore instead? We can tell everyone we've been around the whole island."

Erik could have sworn that the clouds were moving faster than when they'd left Gibsons, but like the others he was thrilled by the speed of the new boat. All of them felt a new power—over the sea, the wind, even over the clouds. It gave them a wonderful sense of freedom and excitement, particularly Mike, who, until two years ago, had been living in Manitoba.

Protected by Bowen's long easterly shore, Mike steered due south until he came to the rocky promontory of Cowan's Point.

"It's rough out there," Erik warned, pointing. "Look at the size of those whitecaps."

The wind was raging past them down Georgia Strait toward the Fraser River delta to the south.

"No problem," said Mike. "This boat can handle that. It's the same distance if we go this way, isn't it?" he asked.

"Yep," nodded Erik. "But rougher. See the swells crashing against the point? I think we should go back the way we came. Now, before it's too late."

Mike shook his head. "I said this boat can handle it."

Erik thought that Mike's lack of boating experience might have given him a false sense of security, but he kept it to himself.

"Maybe we should put our life jackets on," said Dave. But no one did.

As Mike steered out past the point, he reduced speed. The

waves were now higher than their windshield and they were forced to hold onto the seats. For the first five minutes, as they cut through the top of each breaker and slammed down into the troughs, they enjoyed themselves, screaming and laughing. It was only water, after all. They had swum in it every day that past summer, diving with their friends off the sheltered Hopkins wharf, chasing each other like seals under Erik's father's boat and floats, taking turns towing one another behind *DC-3* on inner tubes or boards.

The wind had been blowing unimpeded down the open strait for a hundred miles or more. Gaining momentum as it tore along, it dragged the water in its invisible grasp, building the swells higher and longer. It blew the tops off the waves, some of which were now over six feet high. Spray flew into the boat, and soon the bilge was filled with at least two inches of seawater. Erik began to bail with an ice-cream bucket. Each time the boat flew off the top of a swell and crashed into a trough he had to hold on.

Big Dave began to look worried. He found a life jacket and put it on. "Don't you think we should go back?" he shouted to Mike.

Erik shook his head. "Too late now. Waves would be chasing us. Keep going." Cold seawater sloshed over the windshield, soaking all of them. Erik grabbed the other two life jackets and handed one to Mike. They both zipped them up without comment.

Mike yelled, "How much further?"

"Couple of miles," said Erik pointing toward the next rocky point, "then turn starboard round Cape Roger Curtis."

But against Erik's advice, Mike wheeled the boat around, back toward Cowan's Point. None of them were prepared for what happened next.

A six-footer curled over the stern of the boat, partly filling it. Erik worked furiously with the bucket. "See?" he yelled, angry with Mike. "I told you not to turn back." Seconds later, another breaker, a half foot higher, hit them square from behind. "Dave!" he screamed. "Help! I can't keep up!" They soon realized that the following swells were traveling faster than they were. And there was no windshield at their stern to deflect the breakers that were rolling straight over the engine and into the boat.

Dave stood there, stunned and scared helpless. "Where's another…?"

"Find a freakin' pan or something. Anything!" Erik shouted, his voice breaking. "Your hat!"

Dave fell backward over the seat as another wall of water drenched the boat. Recovering, he grabbed his wet, closely woven hat from under the bow and began to bail. "Jesus! We're gonna sink! We're gonna drown!" he bawled.

"Shut up, Dave! Bail!" Erik yelled. "Mike, turn round again! Head into the wind. Head for the point!"

"Back into that?" Mike shouted. "You're crazy!"

"It's the only way. We can't keep up with this! Hurry."

"For Christ's sake, we've had it either way!" Unconvinced, Mike refused to turn, persisting in steering away from the storm while Dave watched helplessly. Erik poked the disheartened bailer. "C'mon, Dave! Use your muscles!" he ordered, clambering toward Mike. Grabbing the wheel he forced a gradual maneuver. "Turn the boat!" he bellowed, his voice cracking with exasperation. "Can't you see what's happening?"

Mike relented, steered once more into the oncoming waves and wind. "Okay! Okay!" he screamed. "I'm doing it!"

They could seldom see the horizon ahead because of the almost constant wall of water, but like a warning of what could happen to them if they blew ashore, the foaming breakers against the rocky coastline to the starboard stayed clearly within their sight.

As the boat headed back into the wind, Dave and Erik had only one thought. Bail or drown. At least the water level in the bilge wasn't gaining on them. They swore continuously as they worked. Tears of fear and anger were masked by drenching waves. They ignored the jarring thumps that bruised their knees each time the boat landed off a swell. Occasionally it would climb a wave so steep that they would have to grip tightly onto the seats to save themselves from being tipped out.

Mike, meanwhile, was gradually and intuitively learning how to drive into the swells. About half a mile away from Cape Roger Curtis, Erik prodded him. "I'll steer!"

They traded places. As they rounded the promontory to starboard the wind came at them from the port side. Erik pointed toward the gradually lessening swells. "See?" he said, relief in his voice, "the islands are protecting us." He motioned for Mike to take over the wheel again.

Within five minutes they'd almost reached Tunstall Bay on Bowen Island's west side.

Suddenly Dave grabbed Mike. "The engine's on fire!"

They turned to see smoke and flames shooting out from under the outboard cover. For a split second they just stood there, stunned that they should have such bad luck so soon after their last horrible ordeal. Then the engine died.

"What the hell!" swore Mike. "Water!"

Erik seized the bailing bucket, filled it with seawater and tried to lift the cover. "It's too hot!" he shouted, letting it go.

"Throw it up!" yelled Dave, grabbing the bucket from Erik and aiming the water upward under the cover as best he could. For good measure, he threw another bucket before lifting the cover off. The three of them stared in disbelief at the charred wires, water and steam. They wrinkled their noses at the acrid smell. Mike swore.

Meanwhile, the wind and waves blew the drifting boat into Tunstall Bay. Dave, white-faced, leaned over the windward side and started to retch.

"The other side! Or the wind will blow it back in your face," yelled Erik, grabbing him and pulling him leeward in the nick of time. Then he looked at Mike, "It's those rolling side-on swells. Make you barf. Don't feel that great myself."

Dave straightened up. "I'm freezing," he said weakly. "How the hell are we going to get home?"

SALVAGE

THEY were wet, cold and miserable. Even though he realized it would be useless, Mike tried to start the engine. He looked up at the darkening sky and sighed. "My dad's going to be so pissed off with me," he muttered.

Erik suddenly noticed that they were drifting toward the beach.

"Got a paddle?" he asked.

"Under the gunwale," sulked Mike.

Erik felt sorry for him. Even in the best of times, Mike tended to let things get him down, and the boat had made him so happy.

Dave handed the paddle to Erik, who sat on the bow and maneuvered the crippled boat toward one of mooring buoys close by. As he tied the boat to it, he noticed two figures dragging a skiff down the beach. He waved at the young couple who was now rowing out toward them.

"You okay? Need some help?" the man shouted.

"Had a fire. The engine's dead. Could you phone my dad, please?" asked Erik. "He'll tow us home."

"We saw the flames," said the woman. "Scary stuff."

The man wrote down Mr. Johnson's phone number on a piece of scrap paper and rowed back to shore.

"Hope your parents tell ours what's going on," mumbled Dave, frowning. "I'm not looking forward to explaining things."

"Don't worry. They'll just be glad we're alive," Mike said unconvincingly. Erik and Mike knew that Dave was afraid of his dad. When Erik had asked him why, he just said his dad wasn't fair and that his rules didn't make sense.

Erik was also concerned, but for another reason. He remembered the *Snark*'s faulty engine. What if it broke down on the way to Tunstall Bay? Or even worse, on the way back to Gibsons with Mike's boat in tow? Then they'd be in more trouble. He decided not to share this thought with the others.

For the next twenty minutes they all hunkered down close to the bow where it was more sheltered. Even so, they shivered. Dave actually fell asleep, resting his head on a life jacket.

"How many hamburgers could you eat right now?" Erik asked Mike.

Mike sighed. All they'd eaten since lunchtime were a few soggy chips. "Do you have to talk about food?"

"Can't stop thinking about it…I could even eat tofu burgers," said Erik.

Both of them were quiet for a moment as visions of steaming, bulging hamburgers, dripping with ketchup and mayonnaise, hovered before their eyes.

MIKE WAS THE FIRST to speak. "What's taking him so long?" he complained, after another half hour had gone by.

"He should have been here by now," Erik grumbled. "Gibsons is only about four miles away."

About an hour after their boat had first drifted into Tunstall Bay, they heard the sound of an engine. Stiffly, Erik uncurled himself. He recognized the *Snark*'s familiar light pattern. But when he heard how sick the engine sounded, he didn't have the heart to tell his friends to save their cheers until they reached Gibsons Harbor.

Without wasting time on explanations, Mike threw the bowline to Mr. Johnson who fastened it to a long towline. Revving the jet boat engine slowly he held the rpms at a low two thousand instead of his customary four thousand.

Dave complained, "We'll be lucky to get home by midnight at this rate. Can't he go any quicker?"

"Yeah," added Mike. "What's wrong? Doesn't sound as lively as usual."

Erik explained the reason for the *Snark*'s slow speed.

"That's all we need," fussed Mike. "If he breaks down, we'll never be allowed out in the boat again."

Dave nodded. "My dad will freak out."

As if trying to scare them, the jet boat engine coughed, spluttered and caught again, before continuing on.

For the next hour, they were kept on the edge of their seats. Every little variation in the tone and pitch of the engine alarmed them. Each time Mr. Johnson adjusted his foot on the accelerator pedal, the engine faded temporarily, and whenever a swell hit the exhaust outlets in the stern, the engine stuttered, a sound that caused them to catch their breath.

As they rounded Salmon Rock the blinking green harbor light greeted them. Minutes later, Mr. Johnson put the *Snark* in neutral, shipped his towline and maneuvered Mike's boat toward the float beside the launching ramp. With trepidation the boys regarded the small group of parents gathered under the orange street light. Erik could see Mr. Makinen striding toward the float with Mr. Taylor, Dave's dad.

Erik's dad had used the *Snark* to push the stricken boat against the float. He shut off the engine and spoke to Mr. Makinen. "Their outboard caught fire. It might save you a trip if you trailer it straight over to the boatworks for the mechanic to check over."

Mike's dad nodded.

After helping Mr. Makinen load the boat on the trailer, Mike got into his father's truck, Erik climbed into the *Snark* and Dave collapsed into his parents' warm car.

WHILE ERIK WAITED for the hot water to fill his bath, he told his parents—in no more than a couple of sentences—what had happened that afternoon. On his way to the kitchen he overheard his mother say, "I wonder if they'll learn anything from this…"

"Hmmm," grunted Mr. Johnson.

"And you're no better. What would you have done if your engine had quit out there too?"

"You know my attitude to that way of thinking," he answered.

"What's that?"

"Why worry about something that's not likely to happen?"

"And I don't believe in taking chances with an untried engine," she snapped.

"They have to be allowed to make mistakes, to have fun," he argued. "How else will they learn?"

Erik knew his mother wouldn't get far pushing her point of view. Not against his father, the best arguer he'd ever known. He also knew she would have expected her husband to take a chance when it came to rescuing him and his friends. If Mr. Johnson had been overdue because of an engine breakdown, she would have called the Coast Guard or one of their friends who owned a tugboat.

He reheated some spaghetti in the microwave and made a jug of hot chocolate, stirring in a handful each of chocolate chips and marshmallows. He brought a specially made wooden plank out of the laundry closet and laid it across the middle of the bath. After placing his full plate and jug on it, he slid into the hot water, lay there for twenty seconds, then sat up and ate ravenously. Full at last, he lowered his upper body into the water, shut his eyes and began to think about where they could all go next—as soon as Mike's engine was fixed.

AS MIKE AND ERIK opened their school lockers on Monday, their friend Bronya, rushed up, brown eyes flashing. "So what's this about you guys almost drowning out in the gulf Saturday?" she asked.

Toni, willowy, fair-skinned with freckles and long reddish gold hair, caught up with her. "Yeah, Mike," she added accusingly, "how come you didn't let us know you were going out in your new boat?"

"We were in a rush," Mike said. "Anyway, the boat would have sunk with two extra bodies and all that water in it."

Toni glowered at him. "You still should have told us."

"It was no big deal," explained Erik. "We didn't mean to go as far as we did."

"Well, you're nuts," sneered Bronya, running a comb through her dark curly hair. "My dad said you had no business going out on the open strait in that weather."

With the exception of Mike, who'd lived in Winnipeg until he was fourteen, the five teenagers had been friends for years. They had met in kindergarten and had spent the following eight years together in a four-room elementary school. Now at the larger high school, they were still close friends. None of them fit into any of the usual "in" groups and they all felt a little different, as if they didn't belong. They preferred going out on their own, camping, boating, hiking, snowshoeing or tobogganing. More like brothers and sisters than simply friends, they were fortunate to have parents who trusted them enough to let them organize their own excursions to islands and up mountains—as long as they stated where they were going and when they could be expected back. Although they rarely abused this trust, it didn't mean that they didn't get into trouble once in a while.

During the summer holidays Bronya helped her father at his log booming operation in Howe Sound. He'd always given her responsible jobs, starting with labeling the logs when she was ten, to working a 'dozer boat when she was fifteen. That was the job she enjoyed best; she liked to pretend that she was a cowboy corralling cattle as she maneuvered the boat, lurching, twisting and turning like a horse, pushing the logs neatly into their storage booms. Her friends respected the common sense that lay underneath Bronya's tomboyish and fun-loving personality. She was the only girl they knew who could walk on floating logs without falling in.

Both Toni and Bronya were honor roll students, mainly because they worked hard and did their homework. Like Bronya, Toni always had a summer job. She needed to save money for university. The previous year, Toni's mother and father had split up. During that difficult time, she was glad of the company of her friends, but it was Erik she found particularly willing to listen to her troubles.

Bronya finished her lecture as Dave turned up. "Missed the bus," he said breathlessly. "Had to finish my weights."

Bronya glanced up at Dave, who towered nine inches above her. "I'm surprised you could lift anything at all after yesterday."

Dave glared at Erik and Mike. "Who's been spreading rumors?"

Both boys shook their heads. "Parents, I guess," muttered Mike. "They always exaggerate." The bell rang for first period. "As soon as the boat's fixed," he told the girls, "I'll take you out. Promise."

AFTER SCHOOL the next day, Mike and his father went down to the boatworks. While they waited for the mechanic, Erik drove up in his Subaru. He was anxious to see if Mike's outboard had been checked.

"Why did you have to be towed from Tunstall Bay?" Mr. Makinen asked. "I didn't think you would return that way."

"I didn't know the swells would be so big out in the strait," Mike explained.

Erik didn't mention warning Mike not to go that route.

Mr. Makinen shrugged. "Well, if you make a mistake, you have to pay for it...working on weekends. You can help me drywall the house I'm building."

Mike sighed. He hated drywalling, and so did his father. It was heavy, dusty work and it was easy for the pair of them to lose their tempers. It didn't make for a good relationship between them.

At last the mechanic, Steve, arrived and let them into the workshop.

The first thing Erik saw on the workbench was his dad's disassembled 460 inboard engine.

"Hope you're not in a hurry," Steve said. "I've got these to fix before I get to yours." He waved his hand toward three other outboards lying at the back of the shop. "And there's always a chance I might find more damage once I get it apart."

Mike opened his mouth, but his father spoke first. "There will be no rush. He has to earn the money to pay for it first. What caused the problem?"

"Insulation wearing off, shorted out wires, sparks," explained Steve. "That's all it takes to start a fire. And engines and salt water don't mix. Outboards in particular."

"How much is this going to cost?" asked Mr. Makinen.

"Couldn't say for sure till I've got it apart. Two hundred dollars, perhaps two fifty."

Mike's face fell.

"It won't take long to earn that," said his father. "Three weekends—if you stick to it."

Erik, who'd also done a bit of drywalling with Mr. Makinen, sympathized with Mike. Three weekends was a long time, especially drywalling.

ERIK'S DAD'S ENGINE had priority. He needed his boat to make a living and always paid his mechanic's bill as soon as it was presented. Unfortunately, when the new pistons had arrived the previous week, they were the wrong ones and Steve had to reorder them. Even though the second set of pistons came by air freight, the mistake had caused Mr. Johnson's boat to be out of commission for longer than expected. But he wasn't idle. The *Snark*—minus her engine—sat on the trailer in the carport. The boat needed some basic maintenance: a wiring check, bilge pump check, and the largest job of all, a jet bearing rebuild.

At breakfast on the first Saturday since the Bowen Island trip, Mr. Johnson asked, "Do you have any plans today?"

"Not really," answered Erik.

"Great, then you can help me take the jet apart." Mrs. Johnson had always helped her husband with this particular job. Now it was time for their son to learn how to rebuild the bearings.

Half an hour later, they were both hard at work, Mr. Johnson crouching inside the boat with a socket wrench while Erik sat outside on a stool, his nose against the jet outlet and both hands gripping a foot-long screwdriver. While Erik held the bolts still, his dad loosened the nuts that held the jet's back plate in the stern. As they were working, a truck drew up beside them.

Dave poked his head around the stern. "Hi, Erik. Your old man's got you working too, huh? I just snuck away from mine."

"Yes he has," boomed a voice from inside the boat.

Dave grinned. "Oops. Didn't know you were there, Mr. Johnson."

"Looking for a job, are you?" he asked.

"No," said Dave quickly. "Just wondered what Erik was doing."

"Because," continued Mr. Johnson, "if you feel like it, you can scrape those mussels off the jet guard and steering gate. There's a straight-edged putty knife lying around somewhere."

A load of firewood had been dumped in Dave's yard and he knew that if he stuck around his house, his fate for the weekend would have been sealed. So he decided to try mussel removing instead; it sounded cool.

It was a good thing for Dave that the whole hull wasn't covered with them. "These things spatter in your eyes," he complained, working close to Erik. "And they stink."

"That's because they've been dead a few days," Mr. Johnson explained.

At that moment a gob of dead mussel flew out and landed on Erik's mouth. He spat and dropped the screwdriver, narrowly missing Dave's foot. "Yuck! Dave, quit it!" he yelled. "Wait till that stuff gets in your mouth."

Dave laughed so hard he fell off the box he was sitting on. "I didn't do it on purpose," he protested. "Honestly."

"Come on, Erik. Only two more," said his father. "I'm getting a cramp stuck in here."

DAVE HAD ALMOST finished scraping the mussels by the time the two girls turned up on their bikes. "What are you guys up to?" Bronya asked.

"Park your bikes," said Dave, "and I'll show you." As they bent over to see what he was doing, he deliberately stuck the scraper into one of the fattest mussels so that the stinking liquid shot out in the girls' direction. Erik and Dave laughed as Toni got a direct hit on the cheek.

"You're disgusting!" she yelled. Then she noticed how badly it reeked. "Come on," she told Bronya. "It's worse than a sewage plant around here. Let's drop in on the drywallers."

ONE FRIDAY AFTERNOON, in the middle of November, Erik came home to find his parents in the basement.

"Guess what?" his mother said. "I just saw Mike's boat on a test run around the bay."

"Did it look okay?" he asked, his mouth full of banana. "How fast was it going?"

Mrs. Johnson nodded. "Looked fast enough to me."

Erik phoned Mike to tell him the good news, adding, "You can take three in yours, and I'll take one in *DC-3*." They discussed what food and drink they needed to pack. Half an hour later he put the receiver down.

"Sounds as if you're planning a trip," said his mother.

"We thought we'd spend the weekend on Gambier Island," he explained.

"What if the weather's bad?" she asked, remembering the Bowen Island fiasco.

He snorted. "Come on, Ma! Do you think we're wimps?"

"No. But nights are pretty cold at this time of year. And if your sleeping bag gets wet..."

"I wouldn't be so stupid. We'll be okay."

"DAD," SAID ERIK, the following morning. "Are you going out in the boat again today?"

"Why?" asked Mr. Johnson.

"Mike's never been in a jet boat before. He wants to go beach-combing with you."

"How about after lunch?" suggested Mr. Johnson, always willing to take passengers if they were keen. "I only found a couple of logs this morning. It wouldn't hurt to go again." While Mr. Johnson usually welcomed rough seas and howling gales because they knocked the logs off passing booms, he was glad that the weather had been calm during the time his boat had been out of commission. He hated missing out on a log spill. Occasionally a tug captain and his tow of log booms might get caught out in the middle of the gulf in a storm and any number of logs might jump over or slide under the side-sticks. If a boom chain or stick broke, then hundreds might be lost. But satellites and improved weather forecasts had cut down the number of such log spills.

LATER THAT DAY, Mr. Johnson, wearing chest waders and a floater jacket, drove the *Snark*, its aluminum hull gleaming in the sun, up onto the beach below the Johnsons' house. Mike clambered onto the bow, followed by Erik.

"Aren't you going to damage the jet?" Mike asked.

Erik had already explained to him that the jet in Mr. Johnson's boat was a series of three props inside a tunnel that sucked the water through a grid under the hull and shot it full-blast, like an underwater fire hose, through the stern.

"Not if I make sure the grid's clear of the beach before we put it in gear."

Mr. Johnson got off the boat and stood in the water, pushing the bow until the boat was completely afloat. With powerful arms he hauled himself aboard and pointed to a plastic bag floating nearby. "Those bags are bad news for jets."

Once they were settled on the sponge-covered wooden seat, he pulled out the ear protectors from under the bow and handed a pair to each of the boys.

"This engine's a Ford 460," Erik bragged. "It's the same kind the New York cops had in their cars back in the seventies."

As Mr. Johnson drove the *Snark* in a southwesterly direction through Shoal Channel and out into Georgia Strait, Erik leaned across Mike and yelled, "You going to Robert's Creek?"

"Maybe," Mr. Johnson yelled back. He steered a course parallel with the shoreline.

Mike nudged Erik and pointed to a heavily treed ravine that led out onto a rocky beach. "Look, a tent."

Mr. Johnson removed his ear protectors, slowed down and circled offshore. Camouflaged amongst the trees in one of the rare undeveloped sections of waterfront was an old, army-brown tent. Above it, suspended from the trees on either side, was a transparent plastic sheet. A khaki jacket with a yellow chevron on its arm hung over a tree close by and near the logs at the high tide line were signs of a fire. A few empty food and beer cans lay under one of the boulders along with some litter.

"Sharp eyes, Mike," said Mr. Johnson. "It's been there about a week."

"Want to go ashore for a look?" asked Erik.

His father shook his head. "Best not. Anyone living like that around this time of year is probably a little strange. Let sleeping dogs lie." He donned his ear protectors, revved the engine and continued toward Gower Point.

"How fast are we going?" asked Mike.

"Forty knots," said Mr. Johnson, and he stepped on the throttle. "Racing speed…about forty-eight!" After a moment he cut back to his usual cruising speed. "Uses too much gas," he explained.

Erik pointed to a fresh-looking log on the beach. "Dad, a log!"

His father wheeled the boat toward the shore, jumped out onto the rocks and walked up the beach for a closer look before returning to the boat. "No good," he said, shaking his head. "There's rot on the other side."

Further around the corner, where Chaster Creek entered the ocean, lay another log, long and straight with thick brown bark. Looking pleased, Mr. Johnson stopped the boat and removed his ear protectors. "That wasn't there this morning. But it's a bad beach to work on this tide."

"I don't see any rocks," said Mike.

"It's the shallows," explained Mr. Johnson. "The creek's dumped silt and sand way out to sea and it's easy to get beached. Might need two tow lines to reach it," he added. "Don't want to leave it until the tide comes up."

"Or someone else will get it," Erik told his friend.

Keeping his eye on the shallows under the boat, Mr. Johnson steered as close to the beach as he dared and stopped the engine. "Hold the boat with the pike pole," he told Erik, sliding the long aluminum pole with a spike on the top out from under the gunwale and handing it to him. Erik stuck the spiked end into the sandy gravel under the boat and held on so that the strong current wouldn't sweep them further along or toward the beach.

From the side of the boat Mr. Johnson lifted a short length of chain with a hook at one end. The other end was attached to a longer coil of thick rope. With the chain end in his arms, he jumped into the water up to his waist and plowed toward the beach, pulling the rope.

Kneeling near the smaller end of the log, he removed some rocks from beneath it to make a hole and shoved the chain through to the other side. Reaching over the log he took the hook and put it on the chain.

"Is it ready to pull?" Mike asked Erik.

"No. He's going to make it roll down the beach, see? He's sliding the circle of chain around, using up all the chain and circling some rope around. Three times should start it going."

When Erik saw that his father had used almost all the first coil, he got Mike to take over the pike pole while he added another fifty-foot section into the towline, looping the other end of it onto the stainless steel tow post on the stern. "That's a long towline," said Mike.

"It has to be," Erik told him. "Otherwise we can't get a good run."

Mr. Johnson pulled himself into the boat. "Now, when I say hold on, I mean it. I don't want your parents suing me for whiplash or concussion."

Mike shot a puzzled glance at Erik.

Erik nodded. "He means it."

With the long towline connecting the boat to the log, Mr. Johnson drove *Snark* toward the beach as close as possible. Then he turned the boat around to face the opposite way and took off, accelerating the engine's rpms to 2,000…3,000…3,300…4,000…4,500…and… "HOLD ON!" he shouted.

The rope pulled tight with a snap then stretched to its maximum. They braced themselves against the force, which tried to knock them forward against the dash as the boat came to a stop, and then pulled them backward as the tension in the rope loosened. Meanwhile, the log rolled quickly down the beach and hit the edge of the water with a splash. But it was still resting on the gravel in the shallows.

"And again!" yelled Erik, as his father steered the *Snark* toward the log, turned the boat around and took another run the full length of the towline.

"Hold on!" hollered Mike, getting into the spirit of it. Erik was glad to see his normally quiet friend so excited.

This time, as the boat came to a sudden stop at the end of the taut towline, a great deluge of water poured over the stern, slopped up against their backsides and swirled around the floorboards while the boat leveled out. Trying unsuccessfully to hide his alarm, Mike watched Mr. Johnson to see what he would do. But Mr. Johnson just turned the engine off and waited a few moments, his face impassive, unconcerned. The log hadn't moved.

Erik grinned at his friend's expression. He had hoped his dad would do one of those special pulls to give his friend a thrill. "It's okay," Erik said to Mike. "The bilge pump'll deal with it. It's a heavy-duty one, the same type that tugboats use. Moves two thousand gallons an hour."

There was relief on Mike's face as he heard the pump burbling and watched the torrents of water draining beneath his feet.

On the next attempt, Mr. Johnson changed his direction. Starting the run with a little less rpms, he maintained them long after the rope tightened and until the boat had pulled the log into deeper water. He turned the engine off and hauled the towline into the boat. His prize banged against the side of the hull. "Axe and pickup line!" he barked as he unhooked the chain and dropped it noisily into the boat.

Erik handed his father the large, single-bladed axe. From a bin under the seat, he grabbed a fifteen-foot length of half-inch diameter rope connected to a metal spike with an eye at one end. Holding up the spike, he told Mike, "This is called a dog."

"Does it bite?" he asked.

"Yep," said Erik, pointing to a two-inch scar on his father's throat. "One came out of a log once and smashed him and the windshield."

"That's enough telling tales on your father," said Mr. Johnson. "Just for that, you can knock the dog in." He handed the axe back to Erik then turned to Mike. "What's the point in having a son if you can't ask him to do the dirty work?"

Erik steadied the log with the axe blade, placed the point of the dog into the wood—about two feet from the smallest end— swung the axe up in the air with one hand and tapped its heel onto the top of the dog eye. Then, with the dog tip buried only a quarter of an inch in place, he used both hands on the axe handle to drive the dog deeper into the wood. "Should I tie another line into it?" asked Erik.

"Sure," answered Mr. Johnson, digging out a small anchor from under the bow and giving it to him. "May as well leave it here in case we find any more further up."

"How do you know someone won't steal it?" Mike asked.

Mr. Johnson handed him a hammer. "Because you're going to stamp it with my number."

Mike found a smooth spot and thumped it several times with the embossed head of the hammer: LS 608.

Erik fastened the rope to the anchor and threw it overboard.

"Want to take over, Mike?" asked Mr. Johnson, making room at the wheel. "I usually run her at four thousand."

Mike nodded, turned the key and pressed the accelerator with his foot. At first the boat moved sluggishly as the bow lifted, and then as the speed picked up, the boat leveled out and began to plane.

After a dry run to Roberts Creek wharf, Mike turned *Snark* around and cruised back the same way they'd come, picking up the anchor on the way and looping the log's rope over the towpost. As they towed it around Gower Point, they noticed a plume of smoke rising from the shore. Sitting in front of a beach fire near the ravine was a figure wearing the khaki jacket they'd seen earlier. Trying not to appear as though he was rubbernecking, Mike slowed the boat down just enough to sneak a look at the tent dweller. From about two hundred feet away they could tell that the figure was male, perhaps middle-aged, with shoulder-length, darkish, straggly hair, dark eyebrows and a beard. As the *Snark* passed by, the man lit a cigarette, threw the empty red pack into the fire and took a swig from a beer can.

When they were out of earshot, Erik nudged Mike. "Hey, he looks like the stinky guy we saw in your boat at Snug Cove. "

Mike frowned. "Could be."

THE
CAMPING TRIP

AT 9:00 AM the following Saturday, Dave drove his dad's truck down to Erik's house and parked beside the three old Subarus in the orchard. A few minutes later, Bronya's mother dropped off the two girls. Erik was surprised at the amount of food and camping equipment lying on the beach, but he felt sure that they'd need every bit of it.

Everyone sat on a log and waited for Mike, who was fuelling his boat at the gas float in the harbor. The weather was perfect. A little cool, perhaps, but what else could they expect in November? A slight northerly outflow breeze blew down the inlet and into Georgia Strait.

Ten minutes passed. "What's keeping him?" Erik grumbled. To speed their loading operations, he'd dragged his aluminum skiff down to the water's edge, but every now and then he'd have to leave the group to pull it up a few inches because the incoming tide kept refloating it.

"Quit worrying," said Toni. "There's no deadline."

Big Dave began to practice his weight lifting with chunks of driftwood. After managing to move a few fence post-sized pieces, he picked up a hefty-looking block that had been cut off the end of a three-foot-wide log and dropped it close to Bronya.

"Hey, Dave! Watch it!" she yelled.

"Yeah," added Toni. "Quit showing off!"

"I'm not," he insisted. "I didn't get a workout this morning."

Bronya glared at him. "You'll be getting a workout from me if you do that again."

Erik sprang up. "He's coming!" he yelled. He'd spotted Mike's boat tearing out of the harbor, aiming straight toward them. As the boat approached the beach, Mike cut the motor, tilted it up and allowed the boat to drift gently against the shore. Everyone admired Dave's artistic lettering on the bow—*Bailout*, after their first unforgettable expedition.

Erik lifted a cooler aboard. "What kept you?" he asked.

"Dead battery. Dad had to bring another one down."

"How come?" asked Toni, bunching her long hair into a pony-tail with a rubber band.

"The mechanic forgot to charge the old one."

"Typical!" muttered Bronya.

"I guess he thought Mike would do it," said Erik, knowing how easy it was for these things to happen. "Got a bilge pump in there now?"

Mike pointed to the back of the boat.

After a short discussion, they loaded most of the food and equip-ment into *Bailout*. Bronya insisted on traveling with Erik in the smaller *DC-3* because its closeness to the water made her feel she was going faster.

The two boats aimed for Thornborough Channel to the north. As soon as they'd passed the Langdale ferry slip, they steered toward Gambier Island. The bluish green color of the sea changed to an opaque olive green. Huge log booms, sometimes six of them stored side by side along the cliffs, lined the island's north side. Yarding tugs were working on them, organizing them for towing elsewhere, either to the mills, or for resorting. On the mainland side of the channel, boom boats charged around the log storage grounds, making order out of the chaos of a recently dumped barge of cedar logs. Erik sniffed the strong odor of cut cedar in the air. It was a good healthy smell, the opposite of what an overheated classroom smelt like. Spotting another barge about to dump its load, he aimed toward it. *Bailout* followed.

"Stop!" yelled Bronya, waving her arm. She called out to the others in *Bailout*, a few feet behind. "It's the new self-loading barge my dad was telling us about."

Knowing the dangers of a barge dump, she warned them to stay about a quarter of a mile away. They waited patiently as one side of the barge—complete with its own engines and cranes—dipped further and further into the water. The massive pile of logs, lying lengthwise like matches in a box, was aimed toward the side that was sinking. "They're filling the tanks under that side with sea water," she explained.

The logs slid impressively into the sea with a roar and a tremendous splash. The resulting five- and six-foot swells spread out for hundreds of feet. Seconds after their plunge, some of the logs bounced spectacularly up from the roiling water.

"Let's go," shouted Erik, pointing further along the Gambier Island shore to a place free of booms and where the cliffs dropped steeply into the sea.

Both boats sped northward between the black and gray granite cliffs of Thornborough Channel. Erik had to crane his neck to look at the mountainous peaks that rose sharply on each side; their proximity and height made him feel insignificant, almost claustrophobic.

He imagined what his little boat must have looked like to someone watching from the top of the closest mountain.

For a couple of miles he led the others. Then just thirty feet from a sheer cliff face, he signaled them to halt. He turned his outboard off and paddled toward a fern-covered overhanging rock about four feet above his head. "Come and see this," he beckoned. "Watch out for the boulders!" he added as the hull scraped a large submerged rock. "There's a line of them at the bottom of the cliff."

Mike allowed *Bailout* to drift beside the *DC-3*, using his paddle to push against the large boulders that projected out of the water. Erik parted the ferny curtain, revealing a low-ceilinged cave.

"How did it get there?" asked Toni.

"It's been blasted. They were looking for gold," Erik explained. "My parents showed it to me and my sister when we were kids. There are thousands of crickets and spiders on the ceiling. Scared the shit out of me!"

"I'm not scared of that stuff," snorted Dave. "Mike, hold on to the cliff. I'm going in." Digging his flashlight out of his backpack, he jumped onto a rock and crept inside, keeping his legs well bent. They watched as he shone the beam up to the cave ceiling just inches above, before aiming it toward the rear—no more than twenty feet in. Dave held it steady for a few moments. Then he backed quickly and silently outside and jumped into the boat. Wide-eyed, he turned to his friends. "There's something in there!" he half-whispered. "I saw eyes!" He gulped. "I'm not kidding!"

Bronya grinned and pulled her own flashlight out of her bag. "You can't scare me that easily." She climbed over the side of *DC-3* and entered the cave, sniffing the dank air. "Phieeew! What's that stink?" As she shone the light toward the back, a brown furry creature streaked past her and dove into the water by the two boats.

"Otter!" screamed Toni delightedly.

While everyone was having a good laugh at Dave's expense, Bronya gathered a few of the big brown cave crickets in her hands and threw them into Mike's boat. Three landed on Dave's lap. He grabbed them and threw them at Erik who swore and fell backward, causing DC-3 to bounce and bang into Mike's boat, which then hit a rock.

"Idiots!" Erik yelled, frantically tearing his jacket off to make sure the bugs hadn't landed inside.

"Bronya," snapped Mike, looking over the side of his boat to see if the rock had scraped it. "You're an asshole."

"What's the matter? They don't bite," said Dave.

Bronya stood on one of the rocks by the cave entrance waiting to get onboard the DC-3, which had drifted out a bit. "How would I know you guys would freak out like that over a couple of bugs?" she said. "You're a bunch of wusses!"

"I'm not going to get mad, I'm going to get even," growled Erik, starting his outboard. He was furious.

The others laughed. They were glad Mike hadn't thrown the bugs. Only last semester Mike and Erik had been suspended from school for four days for fighting in the lunchroom. A seemingly harmless game of throwing chocolates at each other had turned into an angry thumping match. But when they came out of the principal's office an hour later, they were commiserating over the injustice of their punishment.

"Watch out, Bronya!" warned Toni.

Mike started his engine and joined Erik offshore. Both boats disappeared around the corner, leaving Bronya on the rocks by the cave. She knew her friends wouldn't leave her for long. Anything longer than a few minutes would be considered unacceptable by all of them. When Erik returned to pick her up, he decided to talk to her about the incident—later, when she was on her own, and when he'd calmed down.

Mount Wrottesley loomed ahead, its striking pyramidal shape impressively high and snow clad. As they rounded Ekins Point on Gambier Island and entered Ramillies Channel on their starboard side, they had to shield their eyes from the sun.

Fifteen minutes later Erik slowed and turned the boat into a gravel and rock bay. "We're here!" he shouted. He hoped everyone would approve of the campground.

Offshore, Mike dropped *Bailout*'s anchor.

"Allow lots of line!" called Erik. "The tide will be rising for another hour yet."

After Mike had checked that the anchor had hooked into the gravelly seabed, he waved for Erik who used the *DC-3* to move everyone and their supplies to the shore. Once they were all ashore, they carried the heavy little boat up past the high-tide line.

"Let's eat here," suggested Dave.

But Erik was impatient to explore. "What about climbing the bank first?" he countered. "Let's check out the old farm up there."

"How did you find out about this place?" asked Bronya.

"I came here with my parents years ago to pick plums."

"Well, there aren't any plums at this time of year," Dave pointed out, "so let's eat now. Then there'll be less to carry up that bank."

Everyone, even Erik, agreed that Dave had a point. "But you'll still be carrying it inside you," Erik argued.

"Yes, but it's easier that way," said Toni.

As they ate sandwiches on the beach, Erik remembered picking plums with his sister and mother, while his father, whose hobby was collecting old bottles and other artifacts from abandoned logging camps, had gone off searching for the farm's garbage dump.

He hadn't had enough time to find it, and Erik was anxious to succeed where his dad had failed.

Years ago, a ramp had been cut from the top of the bank down to the beach, but part of it had since fallen away. After lunch Bronya clambered up to the top for a quick scout around. "C'mon," she yelled at the group below. "What are you waiting for?"

Erik was relieved someone else wanted to get going too. He and Dave picked up the big cooler between them and started up the ramp. Halfway up, Dave caught his foot in a root and fell sideways, pulling the chest from Erik's grasp. It tumbled into blackberry brush and jettisoned the pop cans and two cartons of milk into the thickest part.

"Why can't you look where you're going?" Erik shouted.

"How do you expect me to see what's beneath my feet with this thing in front of me?" Dave hollered back.

"Shut up, you guys," Bronya ordered, handing them the empty cooler. "I'll get them."

Erik guessed she was feeling guilty about the crickets.

As she picked her way through the thorny bush to rescue the drinks, Erik took them from her and placed them in the cooler, now safely wedged on the uneven trail. But his extra-long backpack caught in the brambles. Frustrated, he gave a vicious pull and the bushes suddenly let it go. Swearing loudly, he fell backward into the brush, his pack landing on top of him. Mike thought it was so funny he lay on the ground at the top of the bank, kicking his legs and howling with laughter. Erik and the others joined in too, and before long they were competing to see who could make the most noise.

Fifty feet in from the bank, the noisy campers found themselves in the middle of an old, long-forsaken orchard; many of the trees were dead or diseased with rotten limbs and knots of canker. Underneath some lay a few moldering apples. The whole place smelt rather like mushrooms. A clearing with a brick chimney in the middle was the only other sign that people had lived there.

Toni spoke first. "I wonder what happened to the house?"

"Dad said it burned down years ago," Erik told her, "along with the people in it." He took a folding shovel out of his pack and began to poke around the chimney. Under almost six inches of moss and dead leaves, he exposed a layer of charcoal and some concrete under that. "See?" he said. "That's all that's left." He walked toward a mound adjoining a bank about ten feet away and started to dig.

Bronya shivered. "Wonder if they took the bodies away."

"How could they if they were burned up with the house?" asked Dave.

"I'm not sleeping around here," she said. "Let's find another place."

"Ta-dah!" shouted Erik, holding up a cracked canning jar. "It's an old Crown—pity it's cracked." Half talking to himself, he muttered, "This must have been the roothouse." He'd remembered his dad talking about his grandmother's roothouse where she stored the canned food and root vegetables during winter. It had been partly dug into the ground not far from her house to protect the contents from frost.

"Are we going somewhere else, or not?" demanded Bronya.

"What have you got against staying here?" asked Mike.

Dave laughed. "Bronya's afraid of gho-oh-oh-sts," he said.

"I'm not," she retorted. "It just doesn't feel right."

"Okay," sighed Erik, disappointed that they hadn't been more enthusiastic about the place. He was thankful that while they weren't interested in his find, nobody had made fun of him for scrounging around.

"I don't want to lug this stuff all the way back down to the boat," complained Toni.

"Let's try a bit further on," suggested Mike.

"Which way?" asked Dave, looking questioningly at Erik.

He shrugged. "It's up to you. How about through that gap in the brush?" He pointed in a southwesterly direction.

Laden with their equipment, they hiked along the draw that led over to one of the narrow bays on the south coast of the island. They soon discovered a disused logging road that made walking easier.

Bronya caught up with Erik, who'd struck out ahead of the group. "I'm sorry about the crickets," she said. "I'd no idea you had a problem with them."

He was embarrassed. She'd surprised him, bringing the bug-teasing subject up, and he wasn't quite ready for it. "It's not just crickets," he told her, admitting more than he'd intended. "It's all bugs. Centipedes, spiders, anything with bug's legs. When I was two, my sister used to chase me with spiders and shove them down my shirt. She even put them in my bed."

"What a bummer. You'll get over it one of these days," Bronya said. "Lots of people have a strong fear of things like snakes and heights. They're called phobias. My mom's friend won't travel by plane."

"What are you afraid of?"

She was quiet for a moment. "House fires," she said quietly.

"How come?"

She hesitated again. "My grandma almost died in one. She lived in a trailer on our property, and one afternoon it caught fire. My dad rescued her, but I saw her unconscious as he was doing CPR on her. She looked awful. And the trailer was burning down while it was all going on."

Maybe that's why she didn't want to stay around the old home-stead, thought Erik. "How old were you?"

"Four. I guess I ran outside looking for Mom, and when I couldn't find her, I thought she'd been burned too. Turned out she'd gone shopping. She'd left me with Dad."

"Is your grandma still alive?" he asked.

"She lives with my aunt."

Not much further on, Mike and Dave, who were carrying the cooler, stopped and laid it on the moss. Beyond the trees, the late afternoon sun lay mirrored in the calm water of Long Bay.

"How about here?" asked Mike. He pointed to a little stream close by. "Look, drinking water."

"Perfect," said Toni.

Bronya disagreed. "It's too close to the farm."

"Well, we're staying," said Mike with an air of finality.

"Bronya," said Dave, "quit worrying."

Bronya glared at him.

"Crickets, fires and phobias, crickets, fires and phobias," chanted Erik to himself. Then he burped loudly to distract Bronya.

"Erik!" she shouted. "You're gross!"

Dave produced an even louder burp.

"Dave! You're even grosser!" she yelled.

Erik smiled, to himself. Burping was a fun way to prevent a potential argument.

They began to assemble Dave's three-man tent and Toni's smaller pup tent. Erik helped for a few minutes before pulling his shovel and an empty canvas bag out of his backpack. "I'm going back to the farm," he said. "Got some digging to do. Save a job for me to do when I get back."

He knew there had to be an old garbage dump somewhere. Of course, it would be overgrown and hard to spot. He remembered bottle hunting a few years ago with his dad, how they used clues to find the dumps close to where the logging camps had been.

Mr. Johnson had found several collapsed and buried camps, thanks to directions from several old-timers.

Erik stopped at the creek close to where the farmhouse had been and walked a few yards downstream, trying to put himself into the homesteaders' shoes. He thought that they'd probably thrown the stuff near the creek, but closer to the beach so as not to contaminate their water supply. Then he saw a mound in the center of a shallow depression at the top of the bank. That's a likely place, he thought. He decided that if he had lived in the house, that would have been where he would have got rid of garbage.

He dug into the moss and dead ferns on the mound carefully, then moved on a couple of feet and stuck the shovel in—carefully—again. Glass, and soil and charcoal. He bent down, felt under the soil and pulled out a cobalt blue glass bottle. As he held it up to the light, he was startled by a rustle in the forest beyond the orchard.

It was only Mike. "Found anything?"

"Just a medicine bottle," Erik said, handing it to him. "Dad's got four blue castor oil bottles. They're rare. We went up Mt. Elphinstone two summers ago and found an old place—completely rotted flat. I dug underneath and found twenty-three empty opium vials. And some neat old rice bowls and brown soy sauce jugs."

"What do you guys do with all that stuff?"

"It's in our basement. Mom keeps complaining about it, but Dad just tells her to forget about it. He tells her the basement's his responsibility."

"Why would they use opium in the logging camps?" asked Mike.

"Dad said the Chinese laborers led hard lives. Guess it helped their aches and pains." He continued digging a little further away.

"You can tell a lot about people from their garbage. Hey, what's this?" he said, scrabbling around in the soil he'd just disturbed. He cleaned the dirt off as best he could, revealing a metal lantern with a cylinder of discolored glass encircling a smaller cylinder of wire gauze above the oil reservoir. "A Davy lamp!" he exclaimed, handing it to Mike. "See, it says on it."

"Miners used them, didn't they?"

Erik nodded. "That wire strainer thing's something to do with stopping explosions, isn't it?"

Mike looked thoughtful. "Yeah. If there's gas in the mine, a naked flame causes an explosion. The gauze stops the gas from exploding, somehow." He gave it back. "Wonder how it got here?"

"Perhaps someone bulldozed what was left of the house. Shoved it right where we're standing."

Erik and Mike got back to the camp just before dark. "We saved the campfire for you two," Toni told them. Fire lighting was something they both enjoyed. Erik took his portable CD player out of his backpack, turned it on and they set to work.

AROUND TEN O'CLOCK they all turned in. But Dave was not ready to go to sleep. He couldn't resist making frog croaks, burps and other strange noises. Mike began to snore in spite of it, and that prompted Dave to imitate him. Erik joined in, adding what he thought was a convincing snarl of a cougar, then finished his performance with a bear's roar.

"That'll scare them," said Dave.

Bronya yelled. "Why do you guys always make so much noise when we're trying to sleep? You do it every time."

"Move further away if you don't like it," said Dave, knowing that they wouldn't move in the dark, preferring to stay near the fire. Five minutes later, Toni and Bronya, tired of listening to the arguments for and against all-wheel-drive Subaru, Ford Broncos or Chevy 4x4s, pulled out a couple of the boys' tent pegs and collapsed their tent.

The camp was soon finally quiet.

AN HOUR LATER, Bronya woke up. She poked Toni. "What's that noise?" she whispered.

"It's the guys…," mumbled Toni, still half-asleep. Then louder, "What noise?"

Bronya felt for her flashlight. "Listen!" she hissed.

It was a sound so incongruous that for a few seconds it didn't register with either of them; it seemed as if it were part of a dream. Bronya shot out of the pup tent, wrapping her sleeping bag around her. She slapped the walls of the boys' tent. "Wake up! Wake up!"

Toni followed, flashlight on.

Erik, sleeping bag around him and flashlight lit, peered out. "If this is your idea of getting back at us?"

"Shut up and listen!" said Toni.

Mike and Dave crawled out. Everybody stood rigid in the darkness, hardly daring to breathe. Organ music filtered eerily up from an indeterminate direction; the surrounding mountains and rock bluffs deflected the sound. The listeners were silent and motionless as the music continued.

"It's the burned-out farm. It's haunted. I told you we were too close," whispered Bronya.

Toni put her arm round her friend. "No, it's coming from the other way."

Bronya refused to be consoled. "Erik, it's all your fault."

"What do you mean?" he asked.

"You shouldn't have dug up their garbage."

Erik was now convinced that Bronya's overactive imagination was linked to her phobia. "You don't believe in ghosts, do you?" he asked, a hint of incredulity in his voice. He'd always thought she was the more sensible of the two girls.

"Just because you haven't seen any doesn't mean they don't exist," she said.

"True," said Dave. "Just because I haven't seen the Grand Canyon doesn't mean there's no such place."

"But we've seen photos of it!" argued Erik. "No one's taken a photo of a ghost."

"Perhaps the ghosts don't want us to," suggested Toni.

"Sshh!" hushed Mike. "Singing!" A man's voice had joined with the organ music.

"Oh, God," breathed Bronya.

At that moment they heard a rushing sound above their heads and felt a breeze against their faces. Something with gigantic wings had swooped over them. Bronya screamed and dove into her tent, immediately followed by Toni.

Dave shone his flashlight into the closest tree. "It's only an owl," he said. "Looks like a great gray."

Bronya came out of her tent and rejoined the others who had aimed their flashlights into the tree. A huge gray bird barred with dark brown was perched about twenty feet away, its marble-like eyes reflecting green at them.

Dave threw his jacket on. "I'm going to see if I can find out where the music's coming from," he said, sticking a foot into one of his hiking boots. "Anyone else want to go?"

Erik joined him, while Mike stayed in the camp.

Ten minutes later, the two boys returned. "It's coming from Long Bay—about half a mile away," said Dave. "There's a house down there with lights on."

"Pity," said Mike. "I thought it was a ghost-genie from Erik's Davy Lamp."

Bronya sighed and looked at her watch. "Let's get some sleep."

AFTER BREAKFAST they dismantled the tents, packed the gear and hiked back to where they'd left the two boats. Another quarter of an hour's ride south saw them rounding Halkett Point and heading southwest, passing the wide mouth of Halkett Bay. They followed the coastline of rock bluffs and evergreens, past deserted summer cottages, each with a lonely mooring buoy anchored in front. As they approached the unmanned navigation light at Hood Point, they swung their boats to starboard, around the rocks, and entered Long Bay.

Erik shut *DC-3*'s engine off. "Which house do you think it was?" he asked Dave.

"Can't be these," he answered. "They look like summer places. Must be further up."

Three-quarters of the way in, on the port side they saw an old dark green wooden house, the only building with smoke rising from its chimney. A wooden fishboat, even older than the house and painted the same shade of green, was tied up to the float at the end of a ramp that led up to a long, narrow pier. As soon as they'd shut their engines off, they heard the hum of a generator.

"Must be it," said Mike. "They make their own electricity too."

"Let's go visit them," Dave urged.

Bronya shook her head. "But we don't even know them."

"Chicken!" said Dave. "I'll go. Drop me off."

Erik spoke up. "Hold it. I think I know who it is."

"Who?" asked Toni and Bronya together.

"That boat, *Terpsichore*…it belongs to an old guy who used to caretake the log booms when they were stored here a few years ago.

It's an antique. You should hear its engine—a Vivian—just two cylinders. *Ka-putt, ka-putt, ka-putt.*"

"Never mind the boat," said Bronya. "What about the organ music?"

Erik shrugged. "Search me."

"How about coming with me, Erik?" asked Dave.

Erik shook his head. "No way. I don't know him."

Dave looked at the others. "Anyone else?"

No one answered.

"Chicken!" sneered Dave again as they tied up and let him off.

He ambled along the pier, brushing loose bits of peeling green paint off the handrail. Climbing the steps up the steep grassy bank toward the front of the house, he noticed the older wood windows, trimmed with white and set with two rows of rectangular glass panes. Under the house, a windowless basement with a padlocked door had been cut into the bank. The front door was at the top of some wooden steps. There was a hand-carved woodpecker knocker on the door. To the left was a large veranda and a weathered cedar picnic table, on which sat a well-stocked bird feeder.

Dave pulled the woodpecker's string three times and waited. A man with receding gray hair opened the door. He was wearing logger's clothes: blue jeans, a thick red- and black-checked cotton shirt with a green colored down vest, all well used and probably due for a wash.

"Run out of gas, have you?" the man asked, his melancholy brown eyes looking up at Dave through wire-rimmed glasses. From his lined and ruddy complexion, Dave guessed the man must have spent most of his life outdoors.

"Er…no, thanks. I'm Dave Taylor—from Langdale. My friends and I," he pointed to the boats tied up to the float, "we were

camping way up in the forest behind you last night. We thought
we heard some organ music…"

The man smiled. "And you thought you were imagining it?"

"The girls thought it was ghosts, so we told them we'd…"

"Check it out?"

Dave nodded. "Something like that."

"Why don't you go and get your friends so they can see for
themselves?" he said. His speech possessed a gentle lilt.

"You wouldn't mind?" said Dave, feeling more at ease.

"Of course not," the man assured. "It'd be a change to meet
strangers who haven't run out of boat gas. And if they like music,
so much the better."

Dave beckoned his friends from the veranda.

The old man greeted them as they came up the steps. "Hello.
I'm Gareth Davies—Gary to you."

Dave introduced the others.

"So you think there's a supernatural being in my house?" said
Gary.

The girls grinned at each other shamefacedly.

Gary smiled. "You may well be right," he said. "Why don't you
all come in and check it out?"

They followed him into the kitchen, past the woodstove and
into the living room. There was an organ in there, so large that it
left little room for the faded green overstuffed sofa.

"That's it. The best of its kind I could get. Bought it after my
wife died six years ago…Cancer," he added wistfully. "Helps me
pass the time."

"Would you play something?" asked Bronya.

Gary walked over to the organ and turned a switch. "Sure. What
would you like to hear?"

They couldn't think of anything. They were sure that Gary

wouldn't know the music they listened to. And since he spoke with a strange accent, they assumed he wouldn't even know the folk songs they'd learned in elementary school.

"You choose," said Toni. "Play something you like."

"That I will."

Gary's accent reminded Erik of his mother's friend from Wales who'd spent last August with them.

Dave and the two girls settled on the sofa, and Erik and Mike found a space on the dingy braided brown rug.

Gary sat on the organ bench, his slightly hunched back toward them, straggly sparse gray hair brushed against his weather-beaten neck. He opened a tattered book of music and began to play a march. He started off quietly, but halfway through the first verse he added the pedals and more volume. The floorboards vibrated, and during the loud passages the whole house shook. Then to their surprise, Gary began to sing, but no one could understand a word.

When he finished, they clapped and cheered. "What language was that?" asked Dave.

"Welsh," said Gary. "The song is the 'March of the Men of Har-lech.' It's about the Welsh fighting the English to the death and never giving in. I used to sing it when I was your age."

"At school?" asked Toni.

"No. By that time I was working down the coalmines of Rhondda Valley. I lived in a village called Senghenydd, in Wales, and all the miners sang. We had music festivals—miners competing with miners from other collieries." His eyes shone. "You should have heard the hall tremble when all the choirs sang together. All that sound coming deep from the hearts of men. You could feel it in the soles of your feet."

Bronya grinned. "Can't imagine loggers or boom men doing that!"

"They'd be laughed at," said Dave.

"That's their loss," sighed Gary.

"When did you come to Canada?" asked Mike.

"In 1948. Came to visit my aunt and uncle. They'd immigrated and built a house on this island."

"Was your uncle a miner too?" asked Toni.

"For a few years. Then he heard that land was cheap out here... I was twenty when I visited them and never went back to Wales. I became a faller."

"Here?" asked Dave.

"Oh, no. Up the coast. Port Alice, amongst other places."

Toni frowned. "I bet you missed the singing," she said.

"I did. But in one camp there were some Russian fallers who used to sing to an accordion and they taught me some of their songs... But enough about me. You probably want to do some more exploring."

As they trooped through the kitchen, Erik spotted something sitting on a shelf over Gary's woodstove. Usually he would have been too shy to ask, but after his scrounging, he had to know more. "That Davy lamp," he said. "Was that yours?"

"You know what, it is." Gary seemed surprised. "It belonged to my father." He took it down and handed it to Erik.

Erik pointed to the letters B.D. scratched beside the maker's name. "Are those your dad's initials?" he asked.

"Yes. Bryn Davies."

For some reason Erik couldn't bring himself to tell Gary of his recent find at the burned-out homestead.

"Come visit any time," said Gary, opening the door, "even if you do run out of gas."

They all thanked him and promised they would.

"ERIK," SAID DAVE as he caught up to him on Gary's dock. "What else do you know about that guy?"

"Nothing. I just see him going by in that old boat of his doing four miles an hour."

"Where to?"

"Shopping in Gibsons, I guess. But I didn't know he played the organ...Now, that's got power," he enthused.

"Three hours of daylight left," said Mike. "How about Halkett Bay?"

Everyone agreed. "There's a government float in there," Erik told them.

They untied the boats and took off, doubling back around Hood Point—on their port side—past the summer cottages and into the wide bay. At full throttle, Mike and Erik raced the two boats toward the provincial park float and tied across from the only other vessel in the bay, an expensive forty-foot yacht, *Dubious*, whose owners were nowhere to be seen.

Taking their sandwiches and some pop in their pockets, the group walked up the ramp, wandered around the grassy park and hiked half a mile up the hill into the forest. They found a clearing atop a bluff and settled down to eat a late lunch.

"Did you hear what Gary said about his aunt and uncle?" asked Toni.

"Living on Gambier Island?" said Mike.

She nodded. "Yes. Are you thinking the same thing?"

"That Davy lamp," Erik butted in. "It's too much of a coincidence. We've got to visit him again."

"You should have told him about it while we were there," said Dave.

"It didn't seem right. He wouldn't have wanted some strange kids messing about with his relatives' garbage, if they were his relatives. I've got to go back later for another look."

"I wonder how the fire started," said Bronya. "And if it was true about the people being burned alive."

Mike frowned. "He probably wouldn't want to talk about that either."

Erik picked up some rocks and began to throw them at a stump. Bronya placed her pop can on the top and everyone tried knocking it off. When Mike hit it first, everyone yelled and clapped. Suddenly Toni stood and shouted, "Sshh. Listen!"

In the distance they heard a man's voice shouting for help. Scrambling to their feet they tried to figure out the direction the sound was coming from.

"Further up the mountain," said Toni, pointing.

"Let's yell back," urged Mike. "All at once."

"Okay," she said. "After three."

They all hollered, held their breath and listened. When they heard the shout again they paid more attention to its location.

"C'mon, let's go find him," said Bronya. "This way."

THE JACKETS

AS they hiked through the hilly second-growth forest with its patches of brush, Toni reminded them to try to keep two points of reference in view: Hutt Island on Bowen Island's north side and the microwave towers on the top of Mount Gardiner. "And don't forget the direction of the sun," she added.

There were three more shouting exchanges before they came across a bedraggled, unshaven man standing beside a prone, equally bedraggled-looking woman—both of them a few years older than their parents.

"Thank God you found us!" said the man. "We could have died up here and no one would have known!"

Dave muttered to Erik, "Gotta be from the city."

The woman was obviously in pain. She pointed to her left leg. "I think I've broken it," she said. "I fell down that bank."

"We've been here since early this morning," the man continued. "God knows where the dock is. Didn't dare go looking…I'd never have found my way back here again."

"You must be hungry," said Dave.

The stranger nodded. "Yes, but being cold's far worse. Even with these jackets…" He pointed to a mound of moss and dead ferns close by. "We covered ourselves with that stuff to keep warm. Elly's in too much pain."

"That must be your forty-footer tied to the government dock," Erik said.

"We spent the night on it," he said. "I'm Joel Braun, by the way, and this is Elly, my wife."

"Can I have a look at your leg?" asked Toni.

Bronya couldn't help noticing Joel's worried expression. "It's okay. We both took a first aid course last spring."

Toni thought it looked as if Elly might have a simple fracture. At least her leg wasn't deformed and she couldn't see any bone ends poking out. "Get your hatchet out, Erik," Toni said. "I want two smooth straight sticks about two-and-a-half feet long for a splint."

While Erik and Mike were working on two alder branches with a hatchet and a jackknife, Bronya gathered the food left over from lunch—two half-eaten cheese sandwiches and a half-empty bag of chips—and gave it to the couple. Dave donated his full can of Coke.

After the strangers had finished eating, Toni undid the knot at one end of her jacket drawstring and pulled it out. She asked Elly for her red and gold scarf. The two girls placed the two sticks, one on each side of Elly's broken leg, and fastened them with the scarf and string. Their patient winced in pain as they tried not to move the leg any more than necessary.

"Sorry," said Toni. "But I'm sure this'll help."

"But how are we going to get Elly to the boat?" asked Joel.

Dave, Mike and the girls automatically turned to Erik. If they ever had a problem, he always had a suggestion; it didn't necessarily work, but it often prompted someone to come up with a better idea. Erik picked up his hatchet. "My dad says you should always take one of these with you when you're in the forest," he explained to Joel. "And a jackknife."

"We brought nothing," sighed the tired-looking man. "We were only prepared for a short walk in the woods." He laughed ruefully. "We should have known better."

"Don't worry," said Erik, "I've got an idea."

Ten minutes later, he'd cut down two alder saplings and made them into a pair of smooth, five-foot-long poles. "I need two jackets," he said. He chose Dave's and Mike's, shoved the sleeves inside the body and zipped them up. Next, he threaded the poles through the jacket arms to make a simple stretcher.

"This is going to be interesting," said Mike.

With Dave's assistance, Joel helped his wife sit on one jacket so that her legs rested on the other. Mike and Erik took the front, Joel and big Dave carried the heaviest end and the girls led the way down the trail.

The light had begun to fade and lengthening shadows played tricks with their eyes, changing the appearance of certain landmarks they'd noted on the way up. Once in a while the red plane warning lights on Mount Gardiner's microwave towers flashed through the trees, acting as a reference point. But after hiking for ten minutes, Dave became concerned. "I think we're too far east," he said. "I don't remember it being this steep."

"But we didn't have a load when we were coming up," said Erik. At that moment, he skidded on a twig and fell backward, striking the back of his head on a rock and dropping the end of his pole. Joel tripped over him and lunged forward on top of him, while his wife grabbed the other pole with both hands. Fortunately Dave and Mike took most of her weight as she barely managed to keep the injured leg from slamming down. They lowered the make-do stretcher to the ground.

Erik sprang up, apologized and rubbed the back of his head. It felt wet. "Yuck!" he said, seeing blood on his hand.

Joel scrambled to his feet and examined the wound. "It's bleeding quite badly. Any Band-Aids?"

"Haven't got time," dismissed Erik. "Sun's already set."

Once again they organized Elly on the stretcher. "Have you done this hike before?" she asked.

"Nope," said Mike.

"Well, how the hell do you know where you're going?" asked Joel. It was obvious he had little faith in their wilderness skills.

"We do a lot of hiking," answered Toni. "You learn to pay attention to certain things." Even with the girls scouting the easiest route, it was slow going. The stretcher-bearers had to keep stopping to clamber down slopes, over deadfalls and around brush. They had to circle mounds of bushes and dead ferns. Occasionally they changed sides to give their arms and shoulders a rest. An hour after they'd started out with the stretcher, they arrived, exhausted, at the float. There was barely enough light left to see the boards of the dock beneath their feet, far too dark to call for a floatplane.

"You going to Coal Harbor?" asked Dave, who remembered seeing VYC on the boat's stern.

Joel climbed aboard with him and took hold of Elly as the other two boys helped her into the yacht. "Yes. We have a berth at the Vancouver Yacht Club. It'll only take us three-quarters of an hour to get there. I'll have an ambulance pick us up." He helped his wife into the cabin, laid her on one of the upholstered seats close to the steering console and came back on deck. "We can't thank you enough for everything you've done. How much do we owe for your guiding services?" he asked.

Bronya began, "We don't want money…"

Erik gasped. "Oh no! I just remembered! Dad said if we weren't back by sunset, he would come searching."

Mike frowned. "We're in trouble now."

"I'll phone your dad and explain," said Mr. Braun. "What's your number?"

When Mr. Braun came out of the cabin he said, "We're too late. Your mother says he's already gone looking for you. Doesn't he have a radiophone?"

"No. He drives an open boat," Erik explained. "He said if he got one, it'd just get corroded."

Mr. Braun nodded, stuck his hand inside the door and took a business card from the shelf. "Show him this when you get back."

Erik thanked him and put the card in his pocket. Mike untied *Dubious* and pushed the yacht away from the float.

Back in *DC-3*, Erik got his flashlight out and read the card:

Joel Braun, Riverside Marine Supply.
The Biggest Marine Store in Vancouver.
Care for you and your boat.

"No wonder he had an expensive yacht," he said to Bronya.

AS THE TWO boats approached Twin Islands, Erik recognized the *Snark*'s lights approaching and his heart sank. He winced as his father beamed his million-candlepower, handheld searchlight at him from half a mile away.

Seconds later, Mr. Johnson drew alongside his son's boat. "What's your excuse this time?" he barked. "Have you any idea how many worried-parent phone calls we've had to deal with? Why can't you kids organize things better than this?"

"Dad, you wouldn't believe it," Erik began.

Mike stopped on the other side of the jet boat, shouting, "We just rescued two townies in the forest!"

"One had a broken leg," said Bronya. "They were a mess!"

"Tell me later!" said Mr. Johnson. "Let's get home first—before your mother gets mad."

"It's okay. She already knows…," Erik started to explain, but his words were lost as the *Snark* accelerated away.

While Mike, Dave and Bronya took *Bailout* back to Gibsons, Toni and Erik followed Erik's dad in the *DC-3*. As they walked up the beach in front of Erik's place, she asked him, "When do you want to go back to the garbage dump?"

"Weekend after next?" he suggested.

"That'll be great," said Toni.

He wanted to tell her that he was glad she felt the same way as he did about the place, but he didn't want her to think he was interested in her, in case he scared her off. He'd hate it if she left their group. So he kept quiet.

Inside the lighted basement, Toni gasped. "Erik! There's blood all down the back of your jacket. Go to emergency. You need some stitches."

"Okay, okay—but first I've got to check something out." He dug deep into his large backpack, pulled out the Davy lamp that he'd packed in moss and took it to the basement bathroom. He dampened the corner of the towel and rubbed where the maker's name should be. "See that? I knew it!" he said excitedly. "This one's got RD on it, but it's the same make as Gary's."

"Gary's uncle!" she exclaimed.

Mr. Johnson entered the basement and spotted the blood on Erik's jacket. "Have you been trying to kill yourself again?" he asked. "Hold still for a moment while I have a look," he commanded. "Go show your mother. Looks as if you need a needle and thread."

WHEN ERIK ARRIVED home two hours later with five stitches in his scalp, his mother met him in the kitchen, "You must have made a good impression on Mr. Braun. He just phoned from St. Paul's Hospital to make sure you didn't get into trouble for coming home late."

"How's Elly?" asked Erik.

"Waiting for them to put a cast on her leg," she answered.

"I've dealt with Braun's outfit for years," said Erik's dad. "His dad started it during the 1940s."

"You should have seen his boat," said Erik. "Must have cost at least half a million bucks."

SIX DAYS LATER a large box addressed to Erik Johnson and Co. was delivered by courier to the Johnson house. When Erik opened it after school, he found five new bright orange Mustang floater jackets and a note. "From a couple of city folks. P.S. Elly is making good progress." Underneath the jackets were two walkie-talkie radios, the kind with a two-mile range.

"Hm," he muttered. "One for each boat."

He picked up the phone and told Mike about the parcel. "Let's try them out next weekend," he said, "especially if it rains."

"The burned farm?" asked Mike. "We'll all go in *Bailout*."

"Right on. Saturday at ten? You phone Dave. I'll phone Bronya and Toni."

"Hey, guess what? Mom says I can borrow her Bronco to trailer my boat."

"Great. Then we don't have to rely on your dad every time we take it out."

As soon as he'd put the receiver down, Mrs. Johnson said, "This time, please tell everyone to get home before dark. Your father may go along with whatever you do on the water, but I don't always approve," she said, frowning. "He's too soft with you."

"That's because his parents were too strict with him," Erik told her. "He had to sneak behind their backs."

Erik thought he saw a smile on his mother's face.

"WHAT'S THE FORECAST?" asked Erik when his dad returned from his early morning log salvage rounds the following Saturday.

"Rain, rain and more rain," sighed Mr. Johnson. "Good day to put those jackets to the test."

It was just after ten o'clock when the five friends met at the marina. Mike carefully trailered his boat into the water, and then parked in the nearby lot. After leaving the harbor, he steered *Bailout* to port and opened the throttle.

Dave turned to Mike. "Why didn't we wait for decent weather? The rain's beating into my eyes like pellets."

"Because we're testing the jackets, stupid," snapped Bronya, tightening the attached hood around her head. "Face the other way if you don't like it. Or duck down low."

"Try holding your hand on top of the windshield, like this," said Erik. He'd borrowed a pair of his dad's bright red, foam-lined rubber gloves.

"It's all right for you," said Mike. "You've got those special gloves."

Erik crouched below the windshield and pulled them off. "Take these, Mike. You're driving."

Slowing the boat for a ferry swell, Mike thanked Erik and put them on, but he still grumbled. "Dave's got a point. Let's go back."

"Look, you wimps, I want to go digging," said Toni. "So does Erik. And Bronya. Like archeologists."

If Bronya had mixed feelings about revisiting the dump, she didn't say anything.

As they rounded Ekins Point into Ramillies Channel, the rain came down even harder. "It's always worse up here," shouted Erik.

"Why didn't you tell us that before?" yelled Dave as the automatic bilge pump came on.

The disgruntled group entered the little bay and Mike turned off the engine. He looked at Erik. "Okay, smart-ass," he said. "How do I anchor this boat and get to the beach? Or do you expect me to stay out here and wait all day?"

"Try walking on water," Toni retorted.

Erik pointed at a thirty-foot log that projected out from the beach like a long diving board, three feet above the water. The butt was wedged in between some rocks and the smallest end—no more than a foot in diameter—stuck out over the sea. "There's our dock," he said. "It hasn't moved since we were here last time."

Mike stared at it for a moment. "I'm not walking on that."

"You don't have to. I will." Erik often helped boom his parents' salvaged logs and like Bronya, could walk on one if it was afloat. Except that instead of lying in the water, this log was suspended three feet above it. But he knew he'd have no problem balancing.

"What about the tide?" asked Mike.

"It's coming in. In three hours the log will be covered." He looked up to the clouds. "Hey! It's stopped raining."

Mike drove *Bailout* against the beach and everyone jumped off except Erik. He steered it out to the end of the log, shut the engine off and tied the boat up by its bowline. He tested the log by bouncing on it. "Jammed solid," he yelled. After studying the knot, he took his hatchet, a piece of rope and a metal dog out of his backpack and hammered the latter into the log.

"What are you doing?" shouted Toni from the beach.

"I don't trust the bowline. Could slip off." He tied one end of the spare rope to the dog and the other end to the boat's stern, so that the boat had an extra tie-up.

Satisfied with his safety precautions, he stepped nimbly from the bow to the log. His audience cheered. Halfway between the boat and the beach he had the impulse to give Mike a scare. He stopped and began to teeter over the water.

Bronya was the first to shout. "What's the matter, Erik?"

"Can't move. I'm gonna fall…Feel dizzy." He wobbled some more. "Mike, grab my hand. I need help!"

"Go on, Mike," said Dave. "Get out there."

"If I fall in, I'm going home," Mike said. "I'm not dying of hypothermia."

Mike climbed one of the rocks that were holding the log fast, jumped onto it, took two steps out over the water and froze. The others cheered and clapped while Erik laughed so hard he nearly fell in. He ran along the log toward his friend. "I was only fooling," Erik told him. "You look so funny stuck up there."

Mike yelled, "You son-of-a…!" Once they were both off the log, he chased Erik along the beach, up the bank and into the bush, away from where the house stood. But when they saw the others had come ashore, they caught up with them.

GARBAGE

ERIK and Mike led them toward the depression near the creek. Dave, who'd also brought a shovel, started digging about six feet away from Erik. The ash and charcoal was fairly deep in some places and practically nonexistent in others. They found a mixture of items: rusty cans, old bottles—some broken, some whole—cold-cream pots made from milk glass, cracked cups, an old comb, three toothbrushes without bristles, beer bottles and some chipped dishes. Bronya picked out an intact cobalt blue medicine bottle. "Mine!" she said.

Erik uncovered a hand-painted bowl that he gave to Toni because she admired it.

"It's a sugar bowl," she said, stashing it away in her pack.

Dave found an old square cookie tin; its decorative markings had been scorched or rusted away. "Cookies, anyone?" he said, trying to open it. But the lid was stuck. As he shook it he could feel something knocking about inside.

"Here," said Mike, grabbing the box, "I'll get it off." He rattled it. "It's full of spiders. I can hear them." He glanced at Erik and started running purposefully toward him.

Erik, knowing that Mike still wanted to get even, dropped his shovel and hightailed it toward the chimney. "No, you don't!" Erik shouted, before hiding behind the chimney. But Mike caught his foot in an ivy vine and fell, slamming the tin against the chimney bricks.

Erik laughed and came out. By that time Bronya had caught up with them. "Mike, you idiot!" she shouted, looking at the now broken tin. "You get mad at me for throwing bugs and now you're doing it."

"What's your problem?" he asked, pulling himself up off the ground and rubbing his knees. "I opened it, didn't I?"

At that moment everyone's eyes fell on what had fallen out— a bundle of old Christmas cards tied up with string. As Bronya picked the package up, the string disintegrated.

She opened one of the cards. "This one says 'Christmas 1954, To Gwyneth and Richard, from Bronwyn and Davydd.'"

"Welsh names," said Erik. "Check the rest."

"Give me some," said Dave, taking a few from her hand.

"Dave, you're so rude," she said, but she let him have them anyway.

As Bronya looked through her pile, she found an envelope inside one of the larger cards. "Hey, look at this!" she shrieked. The envelope had an uncancelled three-cent Canadian stamp on it. "It's addressed to Gareth Davies in Port Alice, and it's sealed. They've forgotten to send it."

"Or lost it," said Toni.

"They must've put the cards in here just before the fire," Erik suggested.

Mike peered over Bronya's shoulder. Although it had quit raining, the light in the small clearing was dim. "Port Alice," he echoed. "Gary must've been logging there."

"Open it," said Dave.

"Dave, you snoop," she said. "No way."

"If you do that," said Toni, "how will you explain why it's opened?"

"How would he know it wasn't opened in the first place?" Dave pointed out.

"Let's take it to him now," said Erik. "He might tell us what's in it."

"Okay," urged Mike, "before it starts to rain again. Looks like it will any minute."

Hurriedly they took the stuff they'd picked out of the dump and made their way back to the beach. This time, Bronya walked the log and brought the boat ashore.

MIKE HAD BEEN right. As they rounded Hood Point, the rain started to fall again, stinging their faces with long, heavy, icy-cold drops, the kind of rain which would give their new jackets the most severe test. They knew that Gary was home because there was smoke coming out of his chimney and his boat, *Terpsichore*, was tied to the dock.

He opened the door even before they set foot on the veranda. "Couldn't you have brought better weather than this godforsaken stuff?"

"Hi, Gary," they chorused as they trooped in, oblivious of the rain dripping off their new bright orange jackets.

"Drying rack's in the mud room back there," he told them, pointing to the little room at the back of the kitchen where he hung his outdoor clothes. "Then come and sit around the fire," he said, opening the door of the woodstove. "What's this? You all joined one of those posh boating clubs or something?"

They looked puzzled.

"Those jackets," he said. "Look like the ones the Search and Rescue people wear."

"Someone gave them to us," said Dave. "We're trying them out in the rain."

Mike couldn't wait any longer. "We've just found something that belongs to you. It's old."

"We were digging in the garbage dump, but we didn't know it was your aunt and uncle's farm," interrupted Erik.

Gary paused for a moment. "How did you find out where they lived?"

Dave explained, "Remember Erik noticed the Davy lamp, last time we were here?"

Gary nodded.

"Well, we found one just like it—marked R D—at the old garbage dump near where we camped that night."

"Erik's dad collects old bottles—" Toni interrupted.

"And when you told us about your aunt and uncle—"said Dave.

"We wondered if the two lamps were connected, so today we went back there to check out the dump again," said Mike.

Gary took a deep breath. "They did live there, and they died there. I was logging on Vancouver Island at the time. No one knew how it happened, but the house was burned to the ground. They were inside. It was a sad story."

Mike dug into his backpack. "Here," he said, thrusting the envelope into Gary's hand.

"They must have meant to mail it," Erik said.

Gary pointed to the stamp. "Just look at that! Who'd have believed the cost of mailing a letter would go up like the price of land. And even worse, the mail service has gone to the dogs."

"How did the lamp get into the dump?" asked Erik.

"After the cops had been there I couldn't bear to go through their things. I just bulldozed what was left and…"

As he watched Gary struggle for words, Erik regretted having asked the question.

After a moment the old man raised his head slowly and looked at each one of them in turn. "Well, since you people had the decency to bring it to me without opening it, I suppose I'd better put you out of your misery." He opened it, looked at the date on the top of the letter and turned it over to see who had written it. His face paled. "It's from my aunt and uncle," he said. "February 1955. The month before the fire." His voice changed to a whisper. "How did you find it?"

They were taken aback by his reaction. For some reason they'd expected him to be happy or at least to smile and be thankful. Mike, now subdued, let Bronya explain.

"It was inside an old cookie tin in the dump," she said, "with a bunch of their Christmas cards. They must've accidentally mixed it in with them and forgotten to mail it."

Mike dug into his small waterproof pack and pulled the cards out. "Here's the rest."

"Later," said Gary, preoccupied with the letter. They waited in silence while he read it. When he finished he spoke. At first he sounded sad, regretful. "If only I'd got this in time." He quickly became angry. "I could've done something," he growled.

Dave was the only one who dared to ask. "Why? What happened?"

Gary leaned back in his chair. "Remember I told you I was from Wales? And my dad and uncle were miners?"

They nodded.

"When I was eight, there was a terrible explosion in the Senghenyddpit near where I lived. My dad was killed along with many others. Because my mother had to work nights at the pub, my aunt Gwynedd and uncle Richard helped look after me. They had a child of their own, my cousin Bleddyn. He was quite a few years younger than me."

"When did they come here?" interrupted Mike.

"Not until 1946. Bleddyn was a teenager. You see, my aunt had just inherited a little money from her family. That's how they bought the land on Gambier."

Bronya slid her chair a few inches away from the fire. "I'll bet your uncle didn't miss his mining job."

"Anything was better than working in those death traps. It made people sick. They died young."

"Where's Bleddyn now?" Toni asked.

Gary stared into the flames. "I haven't spoken to him for many, many years. It's just as well."

Erik guessed Gary knew a bit more about his cousin than he was letting on. "You don't like him?" he asked.

"He stole his parents' life savings."

"When he was a kid?" asked Dave.

"He was old enough to know better." Accompanied by the crackling fire, Gary reminisced. "I came out to visit them just after my mother died. I thought then that he was strange. Anyway, as I told you, that was when I decided to stay in Canada."

"So does Bleddyn own the land?"

"No. They left it to me, all twenty acres. It wasn't worth much, stuck on the north side of the island with no roads, so I didn't do anything with it." He waved the letter. "This explains why they'd changed their will, leaving everything to me and not to Bleddyn."

"You should've sold it and bought a fast boat," Mike burst out.

Gary smiled. "Now why would I need a faster boat? Old *Terpsichore* gives me a chance to enjoy the beauty around me. When you're my age, you want the world to go slower, not faster."

Erik tried to imagine what his father would say if he was told to slow down, particularly if a competitor's boat was coming around the corner and there was a big fresh log between them.

"No," Gary continued, "I'll keep it until I'm old and decrepit and have to buy a house on the mainland. Then I'll need the money. I'm grateful you found this. It means a lot. Now, how about a cup of tea—or some hot chocolate made with canned milk?"

"And some music?" prompted Erik.

"Why not?" said their host.

After giving them hot drinks, he closed the woodstove door and led them into the living room.

Even though they wanted Gary to read the letter aloud, they were too polite to ask. Erik strongly suspected that Gary had kept something important from them.

IT WAS ALMOST 2:30 when Gary glanced out of the window and said, "Fog's rolling in. It's time you folks were on your way."

Billows of low cloud enveloped the trees across the bay. Occasionally, a swirl would drift down and obliterate the far shore.

"You're right," agreed Mike. "We don't want Erik's dad to come looking for us."

Gary let them out the front door. "You have my permission to dig in the garbage dump any time you want. Who knows what else you might find." he said. "Now you be careful in that fog. Slow down and eyes open!" he warned as they clumped down the veranda steps.

Toni bounced on the ramp that led to the float. "I'd sure like to know what else was in that letter," she said.

Bronya untied the mooring line. "He sure had a lot of bad luck," she said. "Losing his dad first, then aunt, uncle and then his wife." The others agreed.

THE RAIN HAD stopped, but the air was dense with moisture as *Bailout* left the little green dock in Long Bay. Mount Artaban was obscured by a cloud of fog; the ceiling was no more than twenty-five feet above sea level. As they turned out of the long bay to starboard, there was nothing visible except for the sea and Carmelo Point. To the south they couldn't even see the north shore of Bowen—the island off which *Bailout*'s engine had caught fire the previous month.

"Where am I supposed to be aiming for?" asked Mike, looking at Erik.

"The shore between Gambier Harbor and Twin Islands," Erik replied.

"How? When I can't see in this stuff?"

"Use your compass."

Mike looked sheepish.

"Didn't you bring it?"

"It wasn't foggy when we left."

"You never know what the weather's going to do," said Erik, suddenly realizing he was sounding like his mother! When he saw everyone's worried expressions, he relented. "Don't worry. I've got mine."

Toni grinned. Erik's jacket pockets were always crammed with stuff. He stood beside Mike to show him the compass reading. "If we aim southwest, we should hit the beach between—"

"Gambier Harbor and Twin Islands," finished Mike.

Erik nodded. "Right on."

Dave wore his worried look. "How long will it take to get there?"

Erik shrugged. "Ten minutes, maybe."

They all kept their eyes on the water ahead. They could see no more than ten or fifteen feet in front of them and could have been out in the middle of the Pacific Ocean for all they knew. Gradually the fog became thicker.

"I think we should slow down," said Dave.

"Yeah," Bronya agreed. "And watch out for log booms or boats."

"I have slowed down," said Mike, easing off the throttle even more.

"Turn off the engine a moment!" Erik ordered.

"What for?" asked Mike as he cut the engine.

"So we can hear the waves against the shore."

They all listened. Apart from the occasional squawk from a few gulls, everything was quiet, too quiet. They heard a soft swishing, almost like someone breathing, repeated sighs, the sighs of the sea.

"We're close," said Erik. "Maybe three hundred yards off."

"It sounds as if the sea's tired," said Toni.

"It probably is," laughed Dave. "Of us!" as he clambered over the windshield to sit on the bow. "I'll watch out for rocks."

Bronya got an oar out from under the gunwale ready to push them off.

Mike started the engine once more and slowly approached where he thought the shore should be.

"Rocks!" shouted Dave, climbing back over the windshield. Mike had seen them too and put the boat into reverse while Bronya jammed the oar against a vicious looking boulder to prevent a collision. "Where are we?" she asked Erik.

"You got me. Just keep going…parallel to the shore."

A hundred feet further on, Mike yelled, "Duck!" Everyone crouched low and found themselves staring up at the cross-beams of a pier inches above their heads. As they passed underneath and out the other side, *Bailout* scraped one of the support pilings with her gunwale.

"Jesus, that was close," said Dave. "Almost knocked my head off!"

"You would have lost more than that if you hadn't jumped off the bow in time!" joked Bronya. The others laughed with relief. Dave was pale and silent.

"That was Gambier Harbor pier," said Erik. "We're on course."

Mike took a deep breath. "Now what?"

Erik checked the compass and pointed into the fog. "Follow the shore to Twin Islands. It's straightforward from then on."

"Sure beats going clear out of the gap and ending up on Vancouver Island," said Bronya.

"If we didn't run out of gas first," said Toni.

"My dad did that in the fog once," said Erik. "Found himself in the middle of the strait."

"Will you guys shut up?" Mike snapped. "I'm trying to drive."

"You're doing fine," said Toni.

The shore seemed endless. Concentrating on what was to their starboard and what was ahead, they hardly spoke.

At last, Erik recognized the rocky promontory off which the twin one-acre islands lay, joined at low tide, but separated at high tide by a narrow shallow channel. Now they had to leave the Gambier coastline and cross the southern part of Thornborough Channel to the mainland. "I'll take over if you want," Erik offered. "I know where the rocks and reefs are." He traded places with Mike and slowed the boat down as far as he could and still be able to maneuver it. "Could be worse," he muttered. "At least it's high tide."

Once free of Twin Islands, he accelerated and returned the wheel to Mike, who asked, "How far is Gibsons?"

"Three miles," said Erik.

The blast of a ship's foghorn in the distance almost sounded like laughter in their ears.

"That's the three-thirty from Horseshoe Bay," said Toni. "There's loads of time to get across."

"And we'll be home before dark," said Erik.

But about a quarter of a mile further on, *Bailout*'s engine began to stutter and cough. It caught again—for a few seconds—and then died.

FOGHORN

WHY now? Erik thought. Why here, in the fog? The sound of a sick motor always filled him with dread.

"Out of gas?" he asked. He clambered over to the gas tank, lifted it and with difficulty gave it a shake. "It's about half full. Try starting the engine."

Mike swore. The engine refused to catch. He swore again.

"A friend of my dad's has one of these," said Erik, jerking his head in the direction of the outboard. "When the water intake gets plugged, the motor overheats and stalls."

"Then what?" demanded Dave.

"Unplug it and wait for it to cool."

The ferry's foghorn sounded again, a little closer.

"How long?" asked Dave.

Erik leaned over the stern. "Can't remember."

Mike tilted the motor. Bronya felt the screen in front of the propeller leg. "There's a bit of weed stuck in there," she said, pulling it out.

"Erik, take the cover off," Mike ordered.

After double-checking the screen, Erik did as Mike asked. "Try again."

But it still wouldn't start.

"Maybe it's not cool enough," suggested Toni. "Wait a couple of minutes."

Erik shook his head. "We don't want to drain the battery." He felt tense, responsible for this boatload of people. If it hadn't been for him wanting to go to the dump, they wouldn't be in this dangerous situation. It was up to him to find a solution. But right now, he was panicking and getting nowhere. Keep calm. Don't let them know how you feel.

Again they heard the ferry's warning. Mike's face turned into a mask of terror. "Shut up!" he screamed as the blast faded.

"The ferry can't hear you," said Bronya.

"You don't have a clue," Mike shouted at her. "This boat's in the ferry's path and it WON'T GO!"

"Stop spazzing," she snapped. "I'm not stupid."

He left the wheel to look at the now exposed engine.

"Check the gas filter," said Erik quietly. "See if there's water in it."

The first thing that the gas line led to was the filter. Mike examined it. "Looks okay."

Erik agreed, so did Bronya. "Want a flashlight?" she asked Mike.

"Don't need it," he said.

The horn bellowed threateningly. Bronya looked up. "They'll see us on their radar screen, won't they?"

Erik shook his head. "No way. To them we're just a drifting chunk of wood. Even if they did know we were a boat, they wouldn't be able to react in time." The ferry's subsonic rumble sounded to him like an ominous sea monster charging toward them.

"Is the gas line squashed?" suggested Dave.

Toni ran her fingers over it from the tank to the engine. "Nope."

As the seven-thousand-ton ferry headed toward them, they heard the PA system announcing the ship's imminent arrival at Langdale, the message that alerted travelers to return to their cars.

Dave's face paled. "I feel sick."

Toni pulled an oar out from under the bow and handed it to him, pointing to the bow. "Get out there and paddle like hell!" she ordered.

"There's another under the port gunwale," shouted Mike, his head close to the engine.

"Which direction?" asked Dave, grasping the windshield and maneuvering himself onto the bow.

Toni pointed in the direction she thought they'd come from and joined him on the bow with the other oar. The ferry's foghorn blasted deafeningly above its roaring engine. "Paddle...away... from that," she said, grabbing breaths between strokes. Her soaking-wet ponytail clung about her neck like seaweed.

"I hate this," gasped Dave. "It's coming straight for us..."

"Dave, stop it!" She struggled to keep focussed, to resist Dave's fear. "We'll beat it..." She used her whole body to push the blade of wood against the water, willing *Bailout* onward, away from the monster.

Meanwhile, Bronya, ignoring Mike's refusal of a flashlight, was shining hers into the engine.

"Jesus Christ!" shouted Mike. "Wire's worn. It's touching the engine, shorting. Erik! Any ideas?"

Perhaps Steve didn't replace all the wires, thought Erik as he fumbled in his pockets. "Here!" he said, thrusting a Band-Aid into Mike's hand. "Wrap this around it," he said, ripping the back off another one.

Mike tore the paper off and twisted the Band-Aid around the naked wire. "There's not enough room in this hole. I need more light!" He grabbed the other Band-Aid and did the same again.

The ship gave another ear-deafening warning. Erik heard his own voice, unnaturally calm. "If we end up in the water, stay together."

"Paddle!" shouted Dave, from the bow.

"Done!" yelled Mike.

"Dave! Toni! In the boat!"

Toni grabbed Dave's oar and threw them over the windshield. One hit Mike's leg as he leaped over the seat toward the steering wheel. He lowered the propeller into the water and turned the starter. It engaged with a jerk. "Hold on!" he hollered.

Erik dropped the engine cover on the floor. Grasping the underside of the gunwale he crouched against the side of the boat while Bronya dove for the gunwale on the other side. Dave lay spread-eagled across the bow with one ankle caught under the port rail and both hands wrapped around the starboard rail. Clinging onto the windshield's support brace, Toni maneuvered her feet along the port gunwale, falling sideways into the boat and almost knocking Mike. She screamed. A monstrous wave was bearing down on them from their port side, and looming above it, the huge, dark shadow of the ferry.

Bailout was lifted sideways. For a terrifying moment, the huge bow wave tipped the little boat at a forty-five-degree angle and threatened to capsize it. Keeping a vice-like grip on the gunwale with one hand, Erik grabbed the engine cover, which was on its way overboard. As the propeller caught, the boat gained sufficient speed, enough downforce, to keep its keel on the water. *Bailout* climbed the giant wave, flew off the top into the air and slammed down on the other side. Mike hung on to the wheel so tightly that his nails dug into the heel of his hand as he steered along the trough, away from the ferry.

Trying to keep his arm steady, Erik pointed. "That way," he said. Then he replaced the outboard cover.

Dave extricated himself from the bow and clambered shakily into the boat. "Holy shit!" he whispered, once they got turned around. "I thought we'd had it."

"Next time there's a fog," said Mike, "we'd better wait until it lifts."

It only took them another ten minutes to reach Hopkins Landing and from there they followed the shoreline to Erik's house.

"Just keep parallel to the streetlights till you reach the harbor," he said, pointing to the coast road. "I'll phone all the parents."

IT WAS ALMOST dark as Erik entered the basement. His father was getting into his rain clothes. "Just in the nick of time," he muttered as he hung them up again. "It's lucky you've all got a good excuse for being late. Did you run into any trouble?" he asked.

"Not really," Erik answered as casually as he could. "We just took our time." He and his friends had unanimously agreed to keep their latest scare to themselves; there was no point in giving their parents any more to worry about than usual.

"Well, at least you had a compass with you. Even so, I'd rather you didn't go out if there's a fog forecast—what with those ferries and log barges out there…Did I tell you about the time your mother and I nearly got run over by a ferry in the fog? About four months before you were born."

Erik gulped and shook his head as it dawned on him that he'd just survived his second near miss with a ferry.

BLEDDYN

THE next Monday, Erik and the others were at the shopping mall during school lunch hour.

They wandered along, killing time until they had to be back for afternoon classes. Suddenly Dave jabbed Erik in the ribs. "Hey!" he whispered. "Don't look now, but that looks like the guy who nearly ripped off Mike's boat in Snug Cove." He pointed at a disheveled figure not far away.

"What are you looking at?" Toni asked, following their gaze.

"Shh! He thinks it's the guy from Snug Cove," Erik warned before turning back to Dave.

Dave nodded. "Camo hoodie. Long straggly hair. Let's check him out."

Erik hesitated. "I don't want him to see me."

"Chicken!"

"Okay, okay," said Erik. "But I don't like it."

They walked slowly past the bench where the man was seated. Trying to appear involved in conversation, they sneaked glances him. As the unkempt man raised his head and looked in their direction, his eyes met Erik's for a fraction of a second before turning away. There was no doubt about it. Trying to decide why he thought the man was so creepy, Erik put it down to the bushy eyebrows over the dark deep-set eyes.

"Well," said Dave, "is it the same guy?"

"Yes. I don't think he recognized us."

"Looks like an old wino. What do you think, Toni?"

She shuddered. "I wouldn't want him anywhere near me."

The five of them hurried back toward the front of the mall. Outside the drug store they ran into Gary, pushing a shopping cart full of groceries.

"Hi, Gary," said Erik, "what are you doing in town?"

"Hello," said Gary. "Can't stop. Gotta get these groceries loaded into a taxi."

"My Subaru's parked next door," said Erik. "I'll take you to the dock."

"Sure you've got time?" the Welshman asked.

"If I run," replied Erik and tore off to bring his car around to the mall entrance.

While they loaded the groceries and then piled into the station wagon, Gary admired the skull hood ornaments. "There's a pig skull in my yard you can have," he told Erik. "Remind me next time you come over."

Suddenly Dave whispered, "There he is again!" The man from the mall was walking past the car.

"Do you know him?" asked Gary.

"Oh, he tried to steal Mike's boat on Bowen a while ago," answered Erik, turning to look at Gary, who had slid down in his seat and was looking out of the passenger window with his jacket collar drawn up around his face. "Are you okay, Gary?" he asked.

"I don't know," muttered Gary. "That was my cousin, Bleddyn. I'd just as soon he didn't see me."

"What!" exclaimed Erik. "That bum?"

Garry nodded. "That's him."

"We think he's a thief!" he said and told Gary about their trip to Bowen Island.

As they drove toward the dock, Gary told them more. "I've never been able to figure out how his mind works. But from what little I know about him, I suspect he'd do anything to get what he wants. Stay away from him."

Toni leaned forward. "He was the one who stole from your aunt and uncle?"

"He forged my uncle's signature, took all his savings and disappeared, so they disowned him. I had to help them out financially after that."

"Did the police ever catch him?" asked Dave.

"I don't think my uncle reported him. He must've spent all the money, because the next time I heard about him—after the fire—he was working in a marina in South Wales. Then about fifteen years ago, someone from my old village wrote to me that Bleddyn had been sent to jail—robbery with attempted murder. I never had any wish to find out the details."

For a moment nobody spoke. Then Dave asked what the others had been thinking. "Did he have anything to do with the fire?"

Gary never missed a beat. "That occurred to me too. Even more so after reading that letter you found. Apparently Bleddyn had just sent them a threatening letter."

"Saying what?" asked Toni.

"That he was going to get even with them for disowning him. He accused them of misunderstanding him, claimed that he'd reinvested their savings and it wasn't his fault if the investment had gone bad, accused them of caring more for their nephew—me—than their own son, and they'd be sorry. They asked if I thought they should report his threats to the police. But as you know, the letter never got sent."

Dave shook his head. "And a couple of months later they were dead. Sounds pretty likely."

"Would you have come back to Gambier if you'd known?" asked Bronya.

"Of course."

"Bleddyn must have discovered he'd been cut out of his parents' new will before the fire," said Erik.

"Maybe," said Gary. "I just wish he'd stay away." He shook his head.

As they got out of the car by the government dock, Gary looked across the harbor toward the Britannia range. "Look at that fresh snow up there," he said. "That fog must've been a sign of the cold weather coming." There had indeed been a hard frost that night. "Glad you made it home okay," he went on as they bounced down the ramp. "I was quite worried after you left, what with the ferry out there hooting like a banshee."

Erik and Bronya exchanged glances. Dave and Mike placed Gary's bags inside *Terpsichore*'s cabin and climbed back onto the dock.

"Thanks a lot," said Gary.

Erik hung back. "I want to see how you start these Vivians. They're antiques."

"Never mind the engine," said Bronya. "School starts in ten minutes."

Erik shook his head. "Mike will drive you guys back. I'll walk. I'll miss math."

"No way," said Mike. "I'm staying here. Toni or Dave can—"

"It doesn't take long," interrupted Gary as he lifted the engine cover on the deck behind the cabin. With five bodies crowded

around him, he set the throttle lever in the right place, poured
about a teaspoon of gas from a bottle into two little cups—"prim-
ing cups" he called them—one on each of the pair of two-foot-high
cylinders. "I turn this until I feel the compression. Sshh. Listen."
He gave the four-inch-wide, thirty-inch-diameter flywheel beside
them a slow half-turn, bringing it back partway. They all heard
a little sucking sound. "That was the gas being sucked from the
cups into the cylinder." He changed his stance so that Dave had to
move back a few inches. "I give her a good spin," he said, cranking
the flywheel over quickly. The engine started with a chuff-chuff,
almost reminding Erik of a laugh.

When Gary saw Erik smiling to himself, he nodded. "Vivian
engines always sound like that. Now she's ready to go home."

"What if it doesn't start first time?" asked Erik.

"You try again until it does. A Vivian in good condition always
starts first time."

"C'mon," interrupted Toni. "Erik, if you miss math again, Mr.
Jenks will fail you."

"He'll fail me anyway," he muttered. After dropping Gary,
noticeably subdued, off at his boat, they all said good-bye. As
Erik drove off, Bronya made a point of telling him that if he
didn't do something about his noisy muffler, he'd get another
ticket. "You've already had one for speeding, haven't you?" she
reminded him.

THAT EVENING, ERIK asked his dad for more muffler repair
tape.

"Again? How many times is that?"

"Four."

Mr. Johnson thought a moment. "I'll check it out in the morning, but I suspect you'll need a new one."

"Can't afford it."

His parents looked at each other. "How about getting your own log salvage license?" suggested his father. "Then you can pick up your own logs and sell them."

Erik beamed. "I didn't think you'd want me competing with you."

Mrs. Johnson smiled. "You wouldn't. Your boat can't keep up with *Snark*."

"And we could work together sometimes," said his dad. "Many times I've wished I could've been in two places at once."

Erik began to imagine the kind of towing contraption he would have to install on the *DC-3*. It would have to be something that wouldn't get in the way of the outboard. That might be difficult, but not impossible. Every log salvage boat he'd seen was at least four feet longer and two feet deeper than his. Nearly all of them had a high metal post attached to the floor forward of the outboard engine so that the towrope would pass freely over it. His short, shallow boat presented a different set of problems.

After supper he took the flashlight to where the boat lay above the high-water mark and shone the beam onto the transom. There were two strong stainless steel handles bolted to each corner of it for lifting the back end. Those would be useful. He'd need about six feet of half-inch rope to make a semicircle from one handle, around the outside of the outboard motor, to the other. Poly rope would float clear of the propeller, unlike nylon that would sink and probably foul it. But if he tied the log's pickup line straight onto the poly rope, the boat would steer awkwardly and the ropes might rub and wear out. A pulley and eye with a little plastic float attached would work, he thought.

Wherever he stood in the yard or the basement, he could see rope of all types, colors and diameters. But he didn't remember seeing a pulley anywhere. He roamed around the cluttered basement, searching until he found what he needed.

LATER THAT NIGHT, the *DC-3* was ready. Erik couldn't wait until the next day to apply for his license. When he phoned Toni and asked if she wanted to go with him, she didn't hesitate to say yes.

It seemed to take him forever to fall asleep that night.

AT LUNCHTIME THE next day, Toni went with Erik to the Wilson Creek forestry office where he filled in the log salvage application form and paid the hundred dollar fee with the money his father had lent him.

"THERE'S A LETTER and parcel for you," said Mrs. Johnson as Erik dropped his backpack on the kitchen floor. It was the first Monday in December.

He tore the envelope open. "My license!" he shouted, even though she was right beside him. Inside the parcel was a cast-iron stamp-hammer—the license number that had to be stamped onto each log he found.

"There's not much daylight left," warned his mother, knowing exactly what he had in mind.

"It won't take long," he said.

"The numbers on your boat have to be seven inches high and—"

"One inch wide. I know, I know!" he yelled, almost falling downstairs in his eagerness to get started.

Half an hour later Erik caught her peering at him through the beach gate. "Ma! Don't you trust me?" He had black paint on his hands, nose, chin and over one eye as well as on his work overalls.

She said, looking at the lopsided, uneven figures. "Why on earth didn't you use a stencil or draw it with a ruler and pencil first?"

"No time. Anyway, it doesn't matter."

HE FINISHED THE paint job as darkness fell, cleaning up in the basement before inserting a handle in his stamp hammer. He'd often watched his father fixing broken axes and sledgehammers; this operation was identical. From a bin of spares, he chose a hickory handle and trimmed the end of it so that it would fit snugly into the hammer. When he had driven it in as far as it would go, he trimmed off the inch or so of wood that protruded from the other side. He selected a metal washer of suitable size and hammered it sideways into the trimmed, wood-filled hole, ensuring the handle was firmly wedged in.

He picked it up and looked at it with satisfaction. There's no way that wood and metal will ever come apart, he told himself.

HE KNEW HE didn't have time to go out before school the following morning because it wouldn't be light until quarter to eight. But at 3:30, without even stopping for a bite to eat, he and Mike entered the house through the basement door, dressed themselves in warmer clothes and went out onto the beach.

"Where are you going?" shouted Mrs. Johnson from the kitchen window.

"Around Keats!" Erik yelled back as he and Mike pulled the *DC-3* into the water. Three-quarters of an hour later, after almost completing the circuit clockwise, they entered a small bay and nearly collided with an unmanned, white fiberglass speedboat. A fifty-horse Merc similar to Mike's was attached to the stern behind a solidly built towpost.

Erik recognized the LS license number on the side. "That's Al

Anderson's boat," he told Mike. "Hope he hasn't fallen overboard." He steered alongside the drifting boat and cut his own engine.

Mike grabbed the gunwale and climbed aboard. "There's an axe, ropes, the kind of stuff your dad has. And an empty cigarette package. And a cigarette butt…"

"You'd make a good private eye," Erik told him.

Mike lifted the gas tank and shook it. "Feels light. Almost empty. What'll we do?"

"I'll anchor it in front of our house and phone Al." Erik kept hold of the speedboat while Mike jumped back into the *DC-3*. At last he could test his towing rig, even if it wasn't with a log. First he tied a sixty-foot-long line onto the Al's boat's bowline.

"Why that extra line?" asked Mike.

"If you tow something too close to your boat, the wash from the prop works against you—pushes the thing you're towing away from you. With a long towline, most of the wash is gone by the time it reaches the other boat."

He secured Al's boat to the extra mooring buoy that was kept in front of their house and tied the *DC-3* to its stern. His father, who had seen the boys coming, rowed his little aluminum rowboat out to collect them. "Beginner's luck, huh?" he said.

"But no logs," Erik told him.

When Erik called Al he was happy to hear about his boat. "It's been missing since yesterday," he said. "Where was it?"

"Keats. Looks okay, and the outboard's still on it. Where do you usually keep it?"

"In the marina—closest berth to the beach. There's no way it could have got loose on its own. I always use two ropes to tie up."

"Do you smoke?" Erik asked.

Al hesitated. "No, why?"

"There was an empty red cigarette pack on the floor and the gas tank was almost dry."

"I'd just filled it," Al said.

"Did you tell the cops yet?"

"Forget it. They won't catch him. Can I collect it tomorrow?"

"Sure. I'll be at school so phone first to see if my parents are in."

When Erik replaced the receiver, he remembered that the empty pack of Dunhills in the boat was the same color as the one the tent dweller along Gower Point had thrown into the fire.

"WHY HAS IT rained every night since I began mooring my boat out there?" Erik complained at breakfast the next day. Because there was no automatic bilge pump in *DC-3*, he had to row out first thing in the morning to bail her out.

His father came into the kitchen. "You can't have it both ways," he said. "At least you don't have to drag it."

"I know, I know. But it's fluky how it's rained every night for at least a week."

"A boat's like a pet," said his mother. "You have to look after it."

"Hmm," said Mr. Johnson. "I'd say it's a big hole into which—"

"You pour your money," Erik finished.

"Speaking of which, how many logs have you found since you got your license?" Mr. Johnson asked.

"Five, which isn't bad considering I'm in school most of the time."

His father nodded. "Not bad at all. Where are you going on Saturday?"

"Gambier. I'll meet up with the others at Ekins Point after I've worked the incoming tide."

A RAINY SOUTHEASTERLY had been blowing for most of Friday night, but as Erik rowed out to the *DC-3* he noticed that the wind had dropped and the skies had begun to clear. His father had left half an hour earlier to go around the islands.

Erik tried to decide which direction he should go. Thinking that maybe the strong winds from the night before would have blown some logs up from the river and then through Collingwood Channel, off Bowen Island, Erik decided to have a look around Gambier Island. He bailed his boat out and took off.

THE CHASE

STEERING between Twin Islands, Erik followed the shore along Gambier Harbor where Dave had almost been decapitated, and aimed straight for West Bay. There, against the beach, he saw his first log of the day, a large hemlock about two feet through at the narrowest end and thirty feet long. But although it was surrounded by water, most of its weight was resting on the submerged rocks and he knew he'd have to wait for the tide to refloat it.

Should I stay here? he wondered, or should I take a chance on someone else pulling it off while I look for others that are already afloat?

He decided to chance it—for a few minutes anyway—until he'd checked Center Bay, half a mile away. As luck would have it, he found another the same size just around the corner and towed it to his dad's mooring buoy nearby. But on the way back toward his first hemlock he saw Danny, one of his father's competitors, in his dark green log-salvage speedboat. Danny was zooming toward it from the opposite direction.

No one's getting my log, thought Erik, opening the throttle as far as it would go. His little boat thumped and pounded on the smooth swells, literally flying from the tops of each mound of water and slamming onto the next mound or the wide trough beneath with a crash.

Reaching the log only ten seconds ahead of the green boat, he wound his towline around his prize and connected it to his towing rig as Danny, foiled, took off across the bay and around the corner. Even though one stamp was sufficient proof of ownership, Erik hammered his license number on to both ends. There he sat in the *DC-3* with the log connected to his boat by the line, feeling more and more frustrated as he thought about Danny finding logs ahead of him. The ten minutes he had to wait for the rising tide to float the log seemed more like an hour.

Beside his father's West Bay mooring buoy he hammered the dog of a pickup line into the hemlock and stowed the towline before tying the log up. Wasting no time, he started the motor, shoved the throttle open and tore past Center Bay where he could just make out Danny's boat, barely moving, at the far end. Erik aimed for Long Bay instead; the windward shore near its mouth was a catchall for southeasterly blown flotsam.

His hunch paid off. "Paydirt!" he yelled. Floating against the steep rocky bluff was a bundle of about fifteen hemlock logs cinched together with two metal straps. As he stuck the blade of his axe into one of the logs, another log salvage boat—a twenty-two-foot aluminum vessel from Bowen Island—came tearing toward him from the other direction. When the salvor saw that the dinky little boat was actually a competitor, he wheeled his craft around the point and charged off toward Center Bay.

My puny Merc's going to have a hard time towing that lot, Erik thought, as he swung his stamp hammer against each of the logs that showed above the waterline. He tied the long towline into one of the straps and started off toward his dad's closest buoy, about five hundred feet away. By now he'd realized that his father had placed the buoys strategically close to bays where stray logs were likely to end up after being blown there by prevailing winds.

At first Erik thought the bundle was too heavy to pull. Then he remembered his father talking about the time he had to tow a small log boom. "It took a while but once it got going, it was easy," he'd said. Sure enough, after Erik had persisted with the throttle wide open for a couple of minutes, the boat and bundle began to move, slowly picking up speed, although he guessed it was probably traveling no faster than a slow walking pace. Remembering how long it had taken the bundle to start moving, he allowed it to drift when they were short of the buoy, using his throttle and a shortened towline to maneuver it. Concerned that one pickup line might not be strong enough, he tied another into the strap to connect the bundle to the buoy.

Danny's boat came around the corner just as Erik was collecting his towline. Erik thought that Danny must be pretty pissed off. Both boats ran up into Long Bay, past Gary's place. But Erik couldn't stop now. Caught up in the hunt, he reached the far end twenty seconds ahead of Danny. Since there were no more fresh logs to be seen, he doubled back and steered to port, rounding Hope Point, past the summer cabins and on toward Halkett Bay.

Gambier was still on his port side as he wheeled the boat around the corner, but ahead lay Anvil Island. He remembered his father telling him that there used to be a brick factory there at the turn of the century. Perhaps there would be some rare bottles lying around…Another time, he told himself and turned his thoughts toward the Gambier shoreline. Approaching the familiar beach below the burned-out farm, he slowed the boat.

There was at least an hour before high tide; enough time for a bit of digging. Aiming the *DC-3* toward the beach, he shut the motor off and tilted the outboard so that the hull slid onto the rocky gravel. He jumped out and pulled the boat farther up the beach, above the high tide line. After hoisting his backpack on his shoulders, he grabbed his folding shovel from under the seat and climbed the bank. It was odd how this place held an attraction for him; the more he found out about it, the more he wanted to know.

He wandered around the bramble-covered house foundations then over toward the garbage dump. Everything was as he and his friends had left it. As he was about to start digging, he heard the sound of twigs snapping, footsteps in the brush. Quickly he ran in the opposite direction and hid behind some blackberry vines. When he saw a man carrying a gun, his stomach contracted into one hard, tight knot.

Bleddyn, wearing his camouflage jacket, was walking toward the bank that led to the beach.

"Oh, no," Erik breathed. "He'll see my boat." As quietly as possible, he crept toward the bank. Peering through the salal he watched as Bleddyn climbed down to the beach and poked inside the boat before looking around for signs of its owner.

What he did next alarmed Erik even more. Bleddyn dragged the *DC-3* down to the shore and pushed it out to sea.

At first, Erik thought he was dreaming. Then, feeling things were getting out of control, he sternly told himself to calm down. Trying to imagine what Bleddyn was thinking, Erik struggled to understand what was going on. Why would he push the boat out to sea? What would he do when he found the boat's owner? thought Erik frantically. Realizing he needed to keep one step ahead, Erik pulled off his bright orange floater jacket and stuffed it in his backpack. It was far too bright. Fortunately, both his vest and backpack were green.

Before turning away from the sea he looked for his boat. It was drifting northward, but he wasn't sure how the incoming tide and the currents and the wind would affect it when it reached the top of Ramillies Channel. He glanced at his watch, and as quickly and silently as he could, pushed through the brush toward Ekins Point, off which he was supposed to meet his friends within the next hour. He reckoned that if Bleddyn did decide to come after him he'd at least have a head start.

A gunshot startled him. Close by. He froze. His heart beat wildly, his mouth felt dry. Run! he told himself. Then…Stop! Calm down! Perhaps you're imagining he's after you. Perhaps he's just deer hunting…But what if he shot to make me run, to hear where I was…to try to figure out where I'm going…? He wouldn't kill me, would he? Gary said he'd been in jail for attempted murder… I'm not taking a chance. I should be able to outrun him—unless he's been training. That's what they do in jail, isn't it? That's supposed to fight boredom.

Erik thought that Bleddyn might be expecting him to go to Ekin's Point. Sticks out like a sore thumb. Boaters can see it from miles away. I'll cut across to the cave instead. No one knows about it. I'll hide there until Mike comes by.

Following the contour of the forested bluffs above and behind Ekins Point, he tried to figure out where the cave would be. He recalled seeing a steep ravine and waterfall emerging somewhere—he couldn't remember how far—to the east of it. The ravine had made an impression on him at the time because as his eyes followed it back up the mountainside it looked as if a giant had slashed a great gouge down the granite with his dagger. He knew that when he came across the ravine he would be on the right track. Again he stopped, held his breath and listened. Erik couldn't tell where Bleddyn was. The occasional sounds of breaking twigs and crashing bushes were indistinct; the trees muffled them and the rock bluffs caused puzzling echoes. With his throat dry and windpipe sore from panting, he forced himself onward, half-running, half-walking, until, through the trees, he caught a glimpse of log booms on the far side of the sound, and Mount Wrottesley standing proud and white, high above. He stood motionless, trying to hold his breath, ears straining. He heard the sound of rushing water.

How far away? he wondered. Lungs burning, he pushed on through the bushes. Then, without warning, there it was, just a few steps in front of him; its straight, high sides must have directed much of the rushing noise upward so that the water had sounded further away than it was. Wet, mossy granite walls hanging with ferns and huckleberry bush dropped into the torrent which coursed over a wide rocky-bottomed chasm. Steeling himself, he peered down the precipitous mountainside toward the sea.

This must be it, he decided. But it's too exposed. He'll see me easily in here. I've got to get across to the trees on the other side.

The sound of the waterfall unnerved him. He couldn't hear anything else. Hurriedly he hiked downhill until he found an easier crossing point. He lowered himself down the ravine wall, and keeping his eyes on the slimy rocks jutting above the icy water, began to pick his way across the falls. Halfway across he made the mistake of looking over the ledge just three feet to his right where the water plunged downward for what seemed to him at least a hundred feet. He felt nauseous and dizzy. Quickly he averted his eyes. "Hurry! No time to look!" he said aloud, forcing himself to concentrate on getting across.

Clinging onto the huckleberry branches he pulled himself up the cliff-like walls. Now under the cover of vegetation, he felt more optimistic about being close to the cave. It should be easier from here, he thought.

As he began to breathe more easily, he heard the crash of boulders from higher up the ravine. This time, he was able to judge more accurately where the sound was coming from, about three hundred feet above him, he guessed. Further away than he'd expected.

Ten minutes later he arrived at the water's edge. Still searching for the cave, he thought back to when they'd left Bronya standing there, how they'd driven away before turning round to pick her up a minute later. Erik tried to recall what the surrounding shore had looked like. In his mind he saw to the east of the cave a little bay with a strangely contorted, U-shaped cedar trunk leaning out over the water, ferns drooping at its mossy base, salmonberry bushes behind it. Perfect for sitting on, he'd thought at the time.

Taking a chance on being seen, he climbed down onto a rocky point and glanced in both directions. Across the bay to the west was a U-shaped cedar trunk but the crook appeared a little different from how he remembered it—tighter. He kept moving, clambering through the prickly salmonberry brush toward it. Stepping onto the slippery rocks, now a foot under frigid water, he crept along until he almost missed what he'd been looking for. He'd forgotten just how well hidden it was. He hoped that Bleddyn didn't know about the cave.

As he ducked into the dark cave his overactive imagination began to scare him even more. He thought of the spiders and the crickets hanging with their spindly legs on the ceiling just inches above his bowed head. He forced himself to get inside, quickly.

This feels like a movie and I'm my own director, he said to himself. Well, my body will have to do what it's told! Those bugs are just robot bugs, cute things. Now take your pocket flashlight out of your backpack, he ordered. Put your floater jacket on! Crawl to the back of the cave…

He didn't even have time to argue with himself. He figured it was unlikely Bleddyn would be carrying a flashlight, and it was impossible to see the back without one.

As he caught his breath, he imagined the robot bugs crawling, clinging onto the cracks in the granite with their sticky hooked feet. It's nothing compared to a bullet in the brain, he told himself. I'd rather sit here with freezing-cold wet feet and fifty thousand robot crickets crawling all over my clothes and down my neck than have to deal with him. Besides, they don't bite—as far as I know.

His feet were numb. He emptied his the water out of his boots, took off his socks and wrung them out. After rubbing the feeling back in his toes and replacing his damp socks, he wondered if wringing them out had been a pointless exercise. Which is colder? he asked himself, a foot in a bootful of water or a foot in a wrung-out sock? Mike's boat should be passing by in about twenty minutes. Will Bleddyn have cleared off by then?

As he listened to the sea's gentle lapping at the cave's entrance he felt something tickle his face. Resisting an almost overwhelming urge to yell and jump about, he took his glove off and gently pulled whatever it was off his cheek. In the beam of his flashlight he saw a rather dozy cave cricket with long twitching antennae. Is it looking for food? He wondered, suddenly remembering his own uneaten sandwiches. He put the cricket on the knee of his insulated trousers and took the sandwich box out of his backpack. He turned his flashlight on and offered a crumb of bread to the insect. It examined the food and chewed. While Erik had lunch, he watched, fascinated, as the cricket ate too.

After fifteen minutes, he put the bug on the floor with another crumb, crept toward the opening and listened. He could hear the drone of a tug engine from further up the inlet. He realized he would have to come out soon, because he wouldn't be able to hear Mike's distant outboard over that noise. His watch showed 1:00 exactly. Gripping the fern fronds that drooped over the cave entrance, he pulled himself up, head projecting above the ferns, facing west, down the inlet. After looking eastward, he ducked back inside. Bleddyn was standing on a bluff forty feet away. Fortunately he was looking the other way.

Erik's heart beat faster and louder as he returned to the back of the cave. He could hear Bleddyn approaching, dislodging small rocks and crushing twigs and ferns underfoot, cursing at whatever got in his way. Well, I'll soon know whether he knows about this place, he told himself. If he doesn't, the only chance of him finding me is if he walks out onto the submerged rocks below, and I can't see him doing that.

For a moment all was quiet.

He waited another five minutes. As he crept quietly toward the mouth of the cave the sound of a rock clattering onto the ledge below him made him draw back. Seconds after that he heard an outboard; he could see through the fern fronds that it was *Bailout*. He cursed inwardly, wondering where Mike would go when he discovered that he wasn't waiting for him. Erik hoped he'd go round toward the farm and look for the *DC-3* there and then perhaps come back to check the shore near the cave.

The smell of cigarette smoke drifted into the cave. When he heard Bleddyn coughing harshly, Erik knew that he was only three feet above him. He'll take another five minutes to finish it, he told himself. He was right. After hearing more rustling in the undergrowth, he guessed his pursuer had moved on.

Erik waited several more minutes, then crawled out below the cave to look back up the mountain for any sign of movement. More confident now, he turned eastward toward the point. There was a boat coming round the corner toward him, but if it was *Bail-out*, would his friends see him? Why would they look for him at the cave? They knew he hated to go inside it. Besides, they would be looking for his boat, not for him.

How could he draw their attention? Shouting or whistling was out of the question. They'd hear nothing above their outboard's roar, and he didn't want to take a chance on Bleddyn being nearby, gun at the ready. He remembered the walkie-talkie. A few days ago Mike had talked about bringing his on this trip, but Erik wasn't sure if he'd remember. He dug out his own, switched it on, and crept back into the cave's entrance to wait for the boat to come closer. Then, making sure the antenna was sticking outside, he spoke into the radio, "Mike, it's Erik. I'm at the cave."

No response. He tried again. Still no answer. When the boat was about half a mile away from the cave's mouth he tried yet again. He stood on a rock and waved. But the steep mountain behind him had cut off the low mid-winter sun; perhaps his orange jacket wasn't showing up. Perhaps no one was looking.

His heart sank as the *Bailout* passed him at top speed. He thought he could see Dave sitting backward, facing his direction, but the three others were standing in the front facing forward. Then, seconds later, his walkie-talkie beeped. It was Dave. "Is that you on shore in the orange jacket?"

"Who the hell do you think it is?" Erik said angrily.

Immediately the boat wheeled around and zoomed toward the cave.

"Let's go!" urged Erik, clambering into the boat and pushing it away from the rocky shore. "Quick!"

As Mike took off Erik pointed toward the shore due north. "Let's get away from here. That way."

"Where's your boat?" asked Toni.

"Bleddyn turned it loose. He's been chasing me with a gun." He felt an overwhelming need to talk, to explain things, as if that last tense hour of solitude was bottled up inside of him waiting to explode. But he knew there were more urgent things to deal with first.

"Where shall we look first?" asked Mike.

"McNab Creek," he said. A cold breeze had just begun to blow from the Squamish Valley. "Feel the wind?" he said. "If the boat's gone up the inlet it'll blow it toward us."

"What happened?" Toni shouted in his ear.

"Tell you when we've found the boat."

Erik pointed to the low-lying valley entrance below Mount Wrottesley on the mainland. "Try over there, near the salt marshes."

They passed behind the tug and log boom that Erik had heard from the cave. As they approached the marshy grasslands around the mouth of McNab Creek, Bronya pointed toward a boom storage area to the west of the creek. "There it is!" she yelled. "Against the boom!"

Erik tied the *DC-3* to *Bailout*'s side cleat. With both boats lying alongside the boom he told his friends about the chase. "What's he going to do next?" he asked.

"Perhaps we should tell the cops," said Dave.

"He'll just tell them he was hunting deer," said Erik.

Bronya agreed, adding, "And you didn't actually see him chasing you, did you?"

"I heard him. That's enough for me. Besides, why did he shove my boat off?"

"Maybe he wanted to trap you, or see who was snooping around?" said Toni as she untied *DC-3*'s rope. "You spent half an hour sitting in the back of that buggy cave?"

Erik tried not to smile. "If someone's after you with a gun, you don't worry about bugs."

"We should tell Gary he's here," suggested Mike.

"Okay, but we can't stop there for long. It's half past two and my feet are freezing."

THEY FOUND GARY working in the lean-to where he kept his generator. "So, what brings you here?" he asked.

"Bleddyn's on the island," said Dave. "Erik just saw him at the old farm."

Gary frowned. "What the hell he's up to?"

"He set my boat adrift and chased me with a gun over to the north shore," Erik explained. "But I suppose he could've been hunting, and me being there was just a coincidence."

Gary shook his head. "I don't think so. He's up to something. Wouldn't be surprised if he's trying to lay claim to the farm in some crazy way. Squatting, or something like that."

"Maybe he already thinks he owns it," suggested Bronya.

"He always struck me as strange, but now I'm thinking it's something more than that. I think a visit to the police is in order. I'll do it when I go to Gibsons on Monday. I'll take that letter you found with me."

"We'll come and check on you tomorrow," said Mike.

"Thanks, but I'm sure you'll have better things to do. Besides, I don't think he'll bother me."

IT WAS 4:30 when Erik walked into the basement where his father was working on the metal lathe. "Just in time," he commented, backing the cutting tool off the spare bushing he was making for the jet bearing.

"My feet are so wet and cold I'm not even sure where they are. Where's Mom?"

"Towing from Pasley. Get any logs this morning?"

"A couple of hemlock, and a hemlock bundle in Long Bay," he answered casually.

Mr. Johnson beamed. "Good for you! I knew I should have gone there first. That'll pay for your license and your muffler."

"Will you be towing from your Gambier tie-ups soon?"

Mr. Johnson nodded. "Tomorrow. Rather not leave the bundle out there too long—could pull loose."

Erik pulled off his boots and peeled off his wet socks. "Did you get anything around the islands?"

"Eight hemlock. That's why your mother's gone towing…By the way, I was going to tell you yesterday. The hippie tent's gone from Gower Point."

"That fits," said Erik. "He must've moved to Gambier." He told his father about his experience on Gambier with Bleddyn.

Mr. Johnson looked serious. "There were a couple of break-ins along Gower Point Road last month. It was in the paper."

"Oh, yeah? Sounds like he got scared. Moved on."

"You should go into the police station."

"Don't need to. Gary's going to on Monday."

"I think you should too. Tomorrow."

Erik regarded police with a certain amount of unease. "They'll think I'm making things up," he said.

"It doesn't matter. They should be told."

"Okay," he sighed. "I'll go."

"Meanwhile, all of you keep clear of that farm. Crazy people and guns are a lethal combination."

"Don't worry," he reassured his father. "We won't go near it."

"Good." Mr. Johnson restarted the lathe motor. "Now, if you want to score points with your mother, you can peel the potatoes."

With another sigh, Erik picked up his socks and dragged himself slowly upstairs. It had been an exhausting day.

Toni phoned him later that evening. "Are we taking the *DC-3* over to Gary's tomorrow with the *Bailout*?"

"You must've read my mind," he replied. "If we found any logs on the way, we couldn't tow them with *Bailout*. The side cleats are too wimpy. They'd probably tear right out of the gunwale."

"Is it okay if I come with you?" she asked. "I mean...instead of Bronya?"

Erik's heart gave a jump. He wondered if Toni had been impressed with the way he'd overcome his fear of crickets. "Sure. See you here at 10:30. I'll let Mike know."

THE PLAN

SOON after 9:30 AM the next day—Sunday, Erik climbed the steps outside the Gibsons police station. Even though he hadn't broken the law, he couldn't stop the feeling of guilt that crept over him. He was relieved that the officer who greeted him at the wicket was not the same one who'd given him a speeding ticket the previous spring.

The constable listened to him patiently and wrote a few details down, including a description of Bleddyn, the Snug Cove incident, the unreported Anderson boat theft and, most importantly for Erik, the chase.

"Our marine detachment is limited," the officer explained, "so I can't see them spending much time searching the whole of Howe Sound. This man hasn't actually harmed or threatened either you or Mr. Davies. And you haven't seen him commit a crime."

Not unless you count pushing my boat off the beach as one, thought Erik. The constable clicked his ballpoint pen four times and glanced up at Erik. "You say Mr. Gareth Davies is going to pay us a visit?"

Erik nodded. "Tomorrow."

"Okay. We'll see what else he has to tell us."

Feeling better, Erik drove home and waited for Toni. They left on schedule in the *DC-3* and met up with *Bailout* about half a mile south of Twin Islands.

Erik beeped for Mike who'd promised to have the other walkie-talkie on. "Hey, Mike, get Dave to stand on the bow and tell me if he can see anything floating out there." When it came to looking for logs, he knew that an elevation of only a couple of feet made a difference.

Dave checked as far as he could see. "Nothing," he told Mike who relayed the message.

A few seconds later Erik warned, "Watch out! Ferry swell!" Dave crouched down and held tightly onto the rail as a large swell hit *Bailout*. He sat up just in time to see the wave hit the *DC-3*. As Toni fell off her seat, Erik grabbed her with both arms and *Bailout*'s passengers guffawed loudly.

"Ho, ho!" yelled Dave. "I saw that."

"Serve you right if you'd fallen overboard, Dave!" Toni shouted across the water.

Erik hoped no one saw him blush.

AS THE DC-3 approached Gary's dock a few yards ahead of *Bailout*, Toni nudged Erik. "What's wrong with *Terpsichore*?"

"It's low in the water," Erik observed, leaping onto the float and looping *DC-3*'s bowline over a cleat. He opened *Terpsichore*'s engine cover. "Go get Gary!" he yelled, picking up a bucket. "I'm going to start bailing."

While Toni ran up to the house, Mike tied his boat to the float and the three of them climbed out. "Stay off," Erik warned. "Don't put any more weight on her." Unfortunately he had no idea where the now-submerged bilge pump or its automatic switch was. He bailed furiously, wondering if a hull fitting—a pipe that fed water to the engine's cooling system—had come loose.

Gary followed Toni hurriedly down the dock and clambered aboard his boat. "Knew I should have checked on her earlier," he said as he bent down and stuck his arm under the oily water.

Erik jumped back onto the float. "Salt water cooling?" he asked.

Gary nodded as he felt the hull fitting. "Yep. It's okay." After fishing around, he pulled the automatic switch from below the engine.

Gary placed the switch on the deck beside him. He cleaned his glasses against his shirt before having a closer look at the switch. "Both terminals are off…Strange thing, for sure."

Mike leaned over the gunwale and peered over Gary's shoulder. "Hey, looks like they've been cut."

"You may be right, but it's more likely the solder's pulled off those spades." He entered the cabin, brought out a little box of tools and got to work.

"She must have a bad leak," said Dave.

Gary worked quickly with the wire strippers. "Several. Needs a complete recaulking job," he complained. "That's the trouble with old wooden boats."

"You don't think Bleddyn's done it?" suggested Erik. "To try to sink the boat with you in it?"

"Don't see why," he muttered.

"To get his own back on you for inheriting the farm," said Erik.

Toni nodded in agreement.

Gary held up his finger to shush them while he listened to hear if the bilge pump was working. Satisfied, he gave a sigh of relief and slowly straightened up. After checking carefully around the inside of his boat, he invited his young friends up to the house.

They sat around the kitchen table and helped themselves from a big tin of shortbread as their host poured boiling water into the teapot beside the stove. "*Terpsichore* thanks you," he said. "Another half an hour and she would have sunk."

"Why did you call her that name?" asked Bronya. "*Terpsichore*. What does it mean?"

"That's what the old Greeks called their spirit of the dance," he explained.

"She doesn't dance very well for a boat," Mike pointed out.

"Ha!" said Gary. "You haven't seen her in a southwesterly!"

They laughed.

"Gary," said Toni, "my mom wants to know if you want to come over for dinner on Christmas day."

Gary brought the teapot to the table. "Tell her thanks, but I'll be staying here."

"Any visitors?" she asked.

"No. I prefer being on my own…And I don't want people feeling sorry for me."

Erik passed the can of milk across to Gary. "What about your kids?"

Bronya gave him a dirty look. "Don't be nosey," she said, kicking him under the table.

Gary stared uncomfortably at his plate. "We never had any."

"No big loss," Erik returned quickly. "You probably would've spent all your time worrying about them. My parents are always worrying about me."

Gary raised his eyebrows in mock amazement. "I wonder why?"

AFTER TEA, THEY waved goodbye and left their host beside the generator in the lean-to, hooking his spare boat battery up to the charger in case the bilge pump had run the other one down.

Bronya stood on the dock and untied *Bailout*. "Do you think it was Bleddyn?"

Mike shrugged, but Erik nodded. "I think those wires had been cut."

"You're paranoid," Dave argued. "Gary didn't think so. But he sure was cranky today, wasn't he?"

Erik loosened *DC-3*. "I'm going to tell my dad to keep an eye on this place each morning he goes by."

But Dave was still not convinced. "Why would Bleddyn sabotage his boat?"

"Because he wants to get his own back, or he's crazy. Maybe both."

They stood on the float for a moment, mulling things over, until Bronya, bowline in hand, turned to Toni. "You coming back with us?"

She followed Erik into *DC-3*. "No. I'm going with Erik."

"Poor Erik!" howled Dave.

Toni grabbed an empty can lying on the dock beside the tie-up rail, filled it with seawater and threw it on Dave. Forestalling a water fight, Erik started the boat and took off.

When he stopped at Twin Islands to check on his father's tie-up buoy, Toni asked, "Does it bug you when the others make snide remarks about me going in your boat?"

"Of course not," he lied. "I like your company."

She seemed relieved. "Good. I thought you'd rather take Bronya."

"Would you care if I did?" he asked.

"Yes."

He couldn't help smiling. "I'm glad. She's fun and I like her, but she's a bit too bossy for my taste. It's you…"

Bailout suddenly appeared from behind one of the little islands and approached *DC-3*. Dave leaned over the gunwale and aimed a mug of water at Toni as they roared past. But most of the contents landed on Erik, and by the time he'd thought about getting his own back, *Bailout* had already left for Gibsons.

Erik put the outboard in gear. "I'll get you for that!" he yelled.

"Let 'em go," shouted Toni. "We don't need them around."

Moments later, Erik slowed the boat down. "Are you in a hurry to get back?" he asked.

She shook her head. "Nope."

"Good. There's a pair of Harlequin ducks off here. Ever seen them before?"

She told him she hadn't.

"The males are really neat," he said. "Like painted ornaments—lots of colors."

As soon as he'd tied the boat up to the float on Hopkins wharf she moved over to share his seat with him. "It's easier to watch from here," she said.

He grinned, and before he'd had time to think about it properly, he put his arm around her. She didn't draw away.

Half an hour later, they pulled the skiff up the beach and walked to the basement, hand-in-hand. As Erik opened the door for her, she ducked under his arm. They laughed self-consciously at each other.

"Hey," she said, "I've got an idea. We should take some mince pies or something Christmassy to Gary over the holidays."

"What about a cold turkey?"

"Or a whole Christmas dinner?"

"You mean cook it first?" asked Erik. "It's too complicated. Christmas is only a week away."

"If we left here at noon on Christmas Eve day, we could be back before dark."

Mrs. Johnson was in the basement, burrowing in the freezer. Erik wondered if his mother had seen them holding hands.

Erik's mom looked up. "Hello, Toni. There's some extra stew if you want to stay for supper tonight."

"Thanks. I'll just call home and tell them I'll be late."

Erik wanted to hug his mother.

ONCE ERIK AND Toni had told them about it, Dave, Mike and Bronya were all enthusiastic about cooking a full Christmas dinner for Gary. They met at the supermarket to buy what they needed. After filling a shopping cart and paying for it, they left the store and entered the mall. They could see through the skylight that it was almost dark. "Hey," shouted Dave, as they passed the Buck Or Two's table display. "Let's get a couple of table decorations."

He picked up a pair of particularly shlocky angels and made them dance with each other like puppets. "What about these?" he said.

"You're joking," said Bronya scathingly.

"But they're musical angels. See, they've got trumpets."

Suddenly Dave nudged Erik and pointed toward the sporting goods store next door. "Hey! Look in there!"

The plate glass window had been painted with a bearded Santa climbing into a chimney with his sack of presents. Erik peered over Santa's hat beneath the moon. Facing the sales clerk was a long-haired customer carrying a backpack. On the floor beside him were two liquor store bags outlining two bottles in each. The man was wearing a dirty baseball cap and the familiar army jacket. Even from behind, he was unmistakable. Erik, his stomach turning somersaults, darted back to the table. "What's he doing in there?"

Dave marched over to the window and stared brazenly inside.

"Hey, Dave!" called Erik in a loud whisper. "Don't let him see you."

Dave returned to the table. "He doesn't have a clue who I am!" And he took up his private-eye position once more, rubbernecking past Santa's chimney, while the others huddled around the buggy in the closest dark corner they could find—about twenty feet away from the nearest exit.

"He must've come over on the foot-passenger ferry," surmised Mike.

Erik nodded. "That's quite a hike. But if you're addicted to booze…"

When Bleddyn left the store five minutes later, the four figures purposely looked the other way. As soon as they heard the swish and clang of the automatic door, they turned their heads just in time to see him disappear out into the night. Everyone gathered around Dave.

"What did he buy?" asked Bronya.

"Two boxes of shotgun shells."

Erik's stomach gave another lurch. "Hunting season's over," he said.

Dave shook his head. "People who live off the land don't care about hunting seasons."

CHRISTMAS EVE

ERIK was still asleep when his mother shouted down the stairs on the morning of Christmas Eve.

"Erik! Someone wants to speak to you on our phone!"

He leaped out of bed, threw his bathrobe on and picked up the extension in the basement.

"Erik? It's Al Anderson. Remember, you found my boat?"

"Hi, Al. Yes," he said, trying to sound as if he'd been up for an hour.

"It's been stolen again."

"Again?" Erik exclaimed.

"I've just been down to the marina and it's gone. Could you or your dad keep an eye out for it if you go out today?"

"Dad's still out in his boat so there's a chance he might have seen it," said Erik

"I've notified the police this time."

"There's something weird about this."

"You can say that again."

Erik yelled upstairs to his mother about the missing Anderson boat. He wondered if he should go searching in *DC-3*.

"Breakfast?" asked his mother when he came into the kitchen.

"No time," he said, digging out his boots from the mudroom. "Gotta look for Al's boat."

"Wait until your dad comes back. He might have found it already."

Mr. Johnson always worked over the Christmas holidays. He only took time off was when his boat was broken or he was so sick he couldn't walk. Experience had taught him that holidays usually produced more lost logs than average; most salvors took time off, and there was also the chance that the tugboat skippers—in their rush to get home with the log booms—might get caught out by rough weather.

Erik returned his boots to the mudroom. "Guess you're right," he said. He took one of his mother's mixing bowls out of the cupboard, poured himself an oversized portion of Cheerios, covered them with flavored yogurt and topped the dish with milk. "I suspect Bleddyn again."

"What made you think he stole it before?"

"There was an empty pack of cigarettes in it—the same kind he was smoking on Gower Point."

"Has Al phoned the police?"

"Yes." He frowned. "I'm sure Bleddyn's up to something. He was in the mall on Friday."

"What was he doing?"

He spoke with his mouth full. "Buying shotgun shells."

Mrs. Johnson put her cup of coffee down. "Promise me you'll stay away from that man."

Erik wasn't used to seeing her with such a serious expression. "Don't worry. He scares me."

After phoning his friends to make last-minute arrangements, he sat across the kitchen table from his mother and stared out the window. The theft of Al's boat had dulled his excitement about today's trip. He was worried for Gary's safety.

"What's the problem?" she asked. "You're supposed to be happy at this time of the year."

He faked a smile. "Just wondering how Gary's going to take our surprise," he said.

"He'll enjoy it. I'll bet he doesn't really want to be on his own."

Shortly after 10:30, Erik saw a boat in the distance, traveling slowly through Shoal Channel. Using binoculars he could see it was his father towing some logs, but there was no white speedboat amongst them.

He went down the beach to meet him. "You didn't see Al Anderson's boat, did you?" he yelled as Mr. Johnson rowed ashore, shipped the oars and allowed the dinghy to slide against the beach.

"No. Why?" he asked, stepping out onto the gravel.

"It's been stolen again."

"Perhaps Al's taken someone else's logs and they're paying him back," suggested Mr. Johnson.

"I think it's Bleddyn."

"How come?"

Erik explained his theory.

His father nodded. "You could be right, but it's rather circumstantial."

Erik opened the basement door. "I'm off to go get Toni."

"It's a bit early, isn't it? She must be pretty keen on your company to put up with a long bumpy ride in that little boat."

"We're just good friends," Erik assured him.

Mr. Johnson hung up his jacket. "Just kidding. She's a nice girl. Wish I'd had a friend like that when I was your age."

Erik's mood lightened somewhat.

BOTH BOATS MET off Erik's house. He held onto *Bailout* while everyone reorganized the food containers. "Seems funny to have a hot turkey and veggies in the freezer chest," said Bronya. Although the day had started bright and clear, it was now overcast with a slight drizzle. A light southeasterly was blowing and Erik hoped it wouldn't get any worse.

MIKE AND ERIK docked their boats opposite *Terpsichore*. As they were securing their boats, *Terpsichore*'s cabin door opened and Gary emerged on deck looking disheveled "Hi there," he said, stifling a yawn. "What's up?"

"Sleeping on the boat?" asked Dave.

"Yeah."

Mike nudged Bronya and whispered in her ear, "I told you he was worried about Bleddyn sinking his boat."

"Someone stole a speedboat from Gibsons last night," Erik told Gary. "The second time in a month."

"Oh?" he said.

"What did the cops say?" asked Dave.

"They're checking into things," said Gary. "Forget about Bleddyn," he said. "Why aren't you lot at home helping with the decorations?" He turned to Mike. "What's all that junk in your boat?"

"It's our present to you," said Toni. "Happy Christmas Eve!"

"We hope you haven't had lunch yet," said Bronya.

"I haven't even had breakfast," he admitted.

"Well," said Erik. "We've brought you more than breakfast."

When Gary's expression changed to a grin, they guessed he'd caught on.

Relieved, Bronya added, "And we're not doing this just for you. It's for Erik's benefit. He wanted two turkey dinners."

"It's partly to thank you for playing the organ for us," said Dave.

"And we were hoping you'd play for us today too," added Erik.

Gary laughed and told them to load up the four-wheeled buggy that he used to transport his groceries and supplies up to the house. Bronya and Dave, followed by the others, pulled the buggy along the dock and up the bank. Gary stopped at the basement door under the veranda, undid the padlock, went inside and came out with a bottle of wine. "This deserves the best," he said, "as long as your parents wouldn't mind."

"They won't. But Erik can't have any," explained Dave. "Last summer he got into the ginseng brandy..."

"And threw up," added Bronya.

"And he hasn't touched alcohol since," said Mike.

Everyone laughed, even Erik.

They followed Gary around the house to the rear door and into the mudroom. "Jackets on the rack, food in the kitchen," said Gary. He stoked the dying fire, stuffing it with more wood before helping the others to lay the table. While Toni cooked the Brussels sprouts, Gary carved the turkey. But when the sprouts were passed around, Gary only took two.

"Don't you like them?" asked Bronya.

"Afraid not," said Gary.

"Neither do I," Mike told him. "I told everyone not to bring them."

Gary passed them to Bronya. "When I was a kid, I used to feed them to the dog under the table until my aunt caught on. After that, she'd shut the dog in the other room until we'd finished eating. If I left my sprouts, she'd use them to make bubble and squeak for breakfast the next day."

"What's bubble and squeak?" asked Dave.

"Leftover greens and potatoes all chopped and fried together in meat fat until they're brown and crisp. Dreadful."

They'd never seen Gary so talkative, so happy. Erik hoped that he was genuinely enjoying himself, that it wasn't an attempt to cover up his concern about Bleddyn's whereabouts. Gary's voice interrupted his thoughts. "Erik! How come you're not having seconds? Don't be polite for my benefit. Come on everyone. Eat up."

"I will," said Erik, helping himself to more of everything. He took a sip of wine from Toni's glass. "This is good."

"Gambier Island blackberry—three years old," said Gary.

"Dave, have some Christmas pudding," offered Bronya.

"There's no ice cream," he complained.

"There's some in the freezer," Gary told him.

"A freezer?" said Dave. "Out here?"

"In the basement. The padlock's undone."

"I'll get it," offered Mike.

Gary complimented Erik on his chocolate cheesecakes. "I'll bet your girlfriend made them."

Erik blushed and shook his head. "No way."

After they'd cleared away and washed the dishes, Gary sat at the organ. "Any requests?" he asked, arranging the cushion on the bench.

"The one about the Welsh fighting the English," demanded Dave.

"The Harlech march," said Mike.

From that stirring tune, Gary segued into one of the saddest melodies they'd ever heard, its plaintive mood echoed by the gray sky and rain.

"What was that about?" asked Bronya after the final chord had faded.

"'Dafydd y Garreg Wen,' or 'The Death of David of the White Rock,'" he told them. "We used to sing it at eisteddfods—Welsh music festivals. But it's supposed to be played on a harp."

"It may be sad," said Toni, "but it's powerful."

Gary nodded. "It is that. And now for something completely different."

Dave started his out-of-tune singing of "Jingle Bells," and the others joined in to try and drown him out.

THEY LEFT AT 3:30 in steady drizzle. The weather promised an earlier than usual nightfall and Erik wanted to check the head of Long Bay for Al's boat. "Besides," he added, "I might find a log or two. It'll only take a few minutes."

"Okay," said Mike. "We'll follow."

"Go with Mike if you want," Erik told Toni. "*Bailout*'s drier."

"Nah, that's okay," she said.

Dave looked at Erik. "I bet it is."

Toni gave him a dirty look. "I'll fix you, Dave," she warned, "with ice water."

Gary accompanied them down to the float. "That was the best lunch I've had in a long time," he said. "I feel strong enough to join the men of Harlech."

He stood in the cabin doorway on *Terpsichore*'s deck and waved as they took off around the point toward the deserted church camp at the head of the bay.

Almost at the camp's float, Erik pointed to a stationary white speedboat about half a mile away, under the shadow of Mount Artaban on the south side of the bay.

"Mike," he said, as soon as *Bailout* had caught up with him. "Isn't that Al's boat?"

"Looks like it," he said, peering through the drizzle. "Want to check it out?"

Erik put *DC-3* in neutral and drifted against the float. "Let's tie here and see if it goes anywhere. We don't want to make him suspicious."

A few minutes later, the white boat sped across the bay toward the west before disappearing around the point in the direction of Gary's float. "See where he's going?" Erik asked the others, concern in his voice.

"Bleddyn," said Dave.

"Let's go after him," said Mike, turning the starter. Nothing happened. He tried once more.

"Not again!" said Bronya. "What's wrong this time?"

Mike shrugged. "You tell me."

Erik leaned over *Bailout*'s gunwale. "Gas?"

"I'm not stupid," snapped Mike. "Where's your flashlight?"

Erik climbed into *Bailout* with his flashlight. "Let's look under the dash," he said.

They both lay on their backs, while Mike shone the light upward into the nest of wires behind the starter. Erik took hold of a single red wire. "This one looks a bit loose," he said. "See? It's almost off the terminal. Got a screwdriver?"

Mike found one in the plastic container he kept in a little corner under the bow. He pulled the wire completely off, scraped it and connected it tightly to the key switch. "That should do it."

But it didn't.

"I'll bet," said Erik, " something else went wrong at the same time."

Dave made a face. "Duh-h!" he said sarcastically.

"I'm serious," Erik insisted. "It's always happening to Dad. He gets so pissed off."

Toni tut-tutted impatiently. "Why do boats break down so often?"

Erik checked to see if the fuel line was kinked. "Salt water corrosion," he explained as he ran his fingers from the tank to the engine. "Salt 'n damp, vibration, pounding."

Remembering their close call in the fog, Bronya removed the engine cover and shone her light inside, while Mike fiddled with a few wires and connections and checked the fuel filter. Seeing nothing amiss, they replaced the cover.

"It's absolutely dead," said Dave. "It's got to be electric."

"Battery," suggested Toni.

Mike shook his head emphatically. "No way."

She shone her flashlight onto it.

"See?" he said. "Both cables are on."

"But look at that one," Toni pointed out. "It's obviously corroded."

Erik leaped toward it. *Why didn't I think of that first?* He removed the terminal with the screwdriver, and Mike scraped all the white and green salty stuff off with his pocketknife before replacing and tightening it.

"C'mon! Hurry!" said Erik.

This time the boat started easily. Erik and Toni climbed back into *DC-3*, and they zoomed off ahead of the others.

"Got your flashlight?" Toni asked him.

"You know me," he said.

FIVE MINUTES LATER, *DC-3* followed by *Bailout*, both running without lights, approached the point near Gary's float. Although it was almost dark and still raining lightly, they could just see the land silhouetted around them. But they almost ran into *Terpsichore* as it drifted on the other side of the rocky point north of Gary's dock. She was listing badly.

Erik grabbed the gunwale. "Hold on, Toni," he said, "I'm going aboard."

The beam of his flashlight showed that the engine cover was off. Even though the bilge pump was working, water was coming in faster than it could cope with. "Don't put any weight on her," he warned as the others drifted close by. "She's sinking fast enough." He knew that this time the leak had been caused by something more serious than loose caulking; *Terpsichore* had looked fine just a short while ago.

Remembering where the hull fitting was located, he stuck his arm though the oily water under the engine and felt the loose end of the rubber pipe only a few inches away from it. "It's been pulled off!" he yelled disgustedly. "There's oil over everything." Fighting the force of seawater pouring through, he slid the pipe back onto the fitting but the hose clamp encircling it was loose. "Screwdriver!" he called to Toni. "In the bucket under the seat!"

She stretched over the gunwale, took his flashlight, and aimed it where he was working, but the beam showed little in the dirty, frigid water. He tried, by feel, to slide the tool into the screw slot of the hose clamp. He knew he had to work fast. His hands and arms were becoming numb. The colder they became, the more sluggish his actions. Three times the screwdriver slipped out, and each time he thought he'd never find the slot again. But once the clamp was tight, he checked the battery that fortunately was still high and dry. The automatic bilge pump was still running; he guessed Bleddyn—for he was certain it was his handiwork—hadn't bothered to disable it, knowing its affect on such a rapid leak would be negligible.

As Erik attached *Terpsichore*'s bowline to *DC-3*'s stern, he told the others, "You three go ahead. Toni and I'll tow. It'll be quieter."

"If Bleddyn's there, we'll cut the engine and paddle in," said Dave, "then we'll check around the house."

Erik started towing at full throttle. As he approached Gary's float, he eased off. He and Toni could just make out the white shape of Al's boat. They watched anxiously as *Bailout* drifted silently toward the dock and their three friends climb onto the ramp. The lighted windows in Gary's house were haloed in the misty rain.

Erik spoke quietly in Toni's ear. "They'd better be careful."

"It's Dave I'm worried about," she whispered. "He might do something stupid to impress Bronya."

She leaped onto the float, grabbed *Terpsichore*'s bowline and secured it to the tie-up rails. Now that the bilge pump had finished pumping and the bilge was dry, Erik replaced the engine cover. He hoped the generator up at the house had masked the sounds of them docking and that it would cover the footfalls and whispers of his three friends as they snooped around the house.

As soon as he'd made sure the rubber boat bumpers were in place, Toni opened the cabin door. She aimed the flashlight's beam at the floor. "Oh my God!" she breathed. "Erik! Quick! Look!"

He stepped over the sill. In the beam of light they saw a body lying facedown between the stove and the stairs. There was a deep gash on the back of his head and a pool of blood beside it.

"It's Gary!" gasped Toni.

Erik knelt to have a closer look. "Is he dead?" he asked. She should know, he told himself. She's taken a first aid course.

She stepped over the body and put her ear close to the side of Gary's face. "He's breathing," she said. She placed her fingers over his neck pulse.

Erik picked up Gary's broken glasses and put them on the table. "Should've got here sooner," he muttered. "I should have left Mike to fix *Bailout* without me…"

"I think the bleeding's stopped," she said.

Quickly Erik drew the curtains across the windows to hide any reflection that might be seen from the house. Very carefully, while supporting his head, they turned him over onto his back.

Toni soaked a towel under the tap, wrung it out and wrapped it around the gash on his head. "You're supposed to raise his upper body if he's got a concussion," she said. "Help me slide those two cushions under his back and head. And he has to be kept warm."

Erik motioned with his head. "Sleeping bag. Over there on the seat."

As they covered him, Gary's eyes flickered open.

"Gary! What happened?" asked Erik.

"Where's Bleddyn?" whispered Gary, fear in his eyes.

"We don't know," Erik told him. "We found *Terpsichore* drifting. The hull fitting was off."

"Bleddyn...," Gary began again. "Tried to make me...sign a will..."

Toni brought him some warm water from the kettle on the stove. "Drink this," she said, holding it up to his lips while he took a couple of sips.

"He must've knocked me out," he murmured.

"He tried to sink the boat to drown you," finished Toni. "He's a murderer!"

Gary winced as he tried to move his head. "Can't move."

"Don't try," she warned. "If you've got something broken, you'll make it worse."

"Where's Bleddyn?" Gary demanded again, then, "Where are the others?"

"They've gone to look for him," Erik told him. "I'm going after them."

"Too dangerous," warned Gary. "He's got an axe. And a gun."

Erik checked the oil stove. "Heat's still on," he said. He turned on the radiophone. "I'll call for help." But when he felt for the mike that usually hung on the unit, he couldn't find it. "Where's the mike, Gary?"

"Overboard...Bleddyn..."

Erik nodded. "I understand. Toni, you stay here."

Gary raised his hand a few inches. "Bleddyn's drunk," he said.

Erik opened the door. "Good," he muttered.

"Hurry up," Toni urged. "We have to get Gary to the hospital—fast."

Before he left, Erik checked the engine compartment again with the flashlight. Everything looked normal.

From the dock, Erik could see that most of the house lights were on, both inside and out. But as he reached the top of the bank, the sight of someone moving about in the kitchen made him duck and hide. Poking his head between clumps of dripping-wet ferns and grass, he watched Bleddyn riffling through the drawers, occasionally taking a swig from the liquor bottle that he kept within arm's reach.

Erik guessed he was looking for cash or other valuables. Gary should've set a rat trap in there, he thought. He was about to go searching for the others around the back of the house, when he saw a figure creep up the front steps, turn left onto the veranda and peer into the living room window.

"Dave!" Erik breathed aloud. Toni was right about him doing something stupid!

When he saw Bleddyn pick up his gun and move toward the door that led onto the veranda, he called out, "Dave! He's got a gun!"

Dave froze; Bleddyn, just six feet away, was aiming it at him. "Take one step and I'll blow your freakin' brains out!" he yelled. "Where's the rest of you?"

"I-I'm on my own," Dave stammered.

"Don' give me that," snarled Bleddyn. "I just heard them!" He pushed Dave toward the edge of the veranda. "Come out you little buggers!" He prodded Dave with the gun.

No one moved.

"C'mon!" screamed Bleddyn. "I'm not waitin' all night!"

As Erik was about to give himself up, Mike and Bronya emerged from the shadows and showed themselves.

"Stay there!" shouted Bleddyn. "If anyone moves, I'll shoot." Sticking the gun barrel into Dave's back, he ordered, "Get goin'! Down there with them!"

"We only came to see…," said Dave.

"Shut up!" Bleddyn snapped, poking him again with the gun.

He pushed Dave down the steps ahead of him and gestured toward the basement door with the gun. "Get in there!"

Once the three of them were inside, he slammed the door, fumbled with the padlock for a few moments, then bolted it before clumping up the stairs into the house. He lay his gun on the dresser and took another drink.

Because the basement had been built as a root house, it had no windows or another door. I'll bet Mike's cursing himself for leaving the padlock undone when he brought the ice cream upstairs, Erik thought, and he wracked his brains trying to think where the key might be. He remembered the blackberry wine. Gary had taken a jangling key ring out of his pocket when he stopped at the basement to get it.

He ran as noiselessly as he could back down the dock to *Terpsichore*.

"Why were you so long?" complained Toni. "Where are the others? I've—"

"The keys!" Erik gasped. "He's got a gun and he's locked them in the basement!"

"Bleddyn?" gasped Toni.

"Jacket pocket," said Gary.

Toni grabbed Erik's arm. "I'm coming with you! Gary, don't move."

Gary motioned them to go with a slight flick of his wrist. "I'll be okay…"

THE PAIR OF THEM lay, huddled together in the ferns and long grass near the top of the bank, watching Bleddyn finish the contents of the bottle. "How long's he been doing that?" asked Toni.

"Long enough."

Several minutes later the sound of a slamming door caught them off guard. Unsteadily, Bleddyn descended the steps with his gun and turned the corner toward the lean-to attached to the side of the house.

Toni nudged him. "Now!"

Erik darted up to the padlock with the flashlight and key ring. He tried at least five of the fifteen keys before he thought of looking at the padlock's make—a Guard. As he fumbled for the matching key, he expected any minute to feel a gun poking into his back. At one point his numb fingers dropped the keys onto the concrete with a clatter. Toni gave him a scare as she sprang from the dark, picked them up and handed them back to him.

He whispered loudly through the latch. "It's me, Erik! I've got the keys."

Hoping Bleddyn couldn't hear anything above the chugging generator, Erik searched frantically through them yet again. Finally one of them worked. He opened the door. "He's in the lean-to," he hissed to the others. "I'm going to get his gun!"

Mike was first out. "You two go that way," he told Toni and Erik, pointing in the direction of the lean-to. "We'll go the opposite way."

"Got it," said Dave.

Erik and Toni crept around the corner and peered through holes in the lean-to's rusty corrugated iron wall. In the light from a naked bulb they could see the double-barreled shotgun lying across one of the forty-five-gallon oil drums near the generator. Bleddyn was removing the cap of a five-gallon red plastic tank.

"Gas?" Toni whispered in Erik's ear.

"Don't know."

Bleddyn sloshed the contents along the house wall at the back of the lean-to, coating the lower five feet of shakes so that the excess fluid pooled along the whole length of the concrete floor.

Then he took out his cigarette lighter.

TERPSICHORE'S WALTZ

E is nuts, thought Erik. He grabbed Toni's hand and fled with her into the bush beside Gary's old garden shed. Any moment he expected a huge explosion.

Bleddyn growled, dug a cigarette out of his pocket, lit it, and inhaled deeply.

"Must've been oil," whispered Erik.

Cigarette between his lips, Bleddyn grabbed his gun. He aimed a flashlight toward the garden shed, fifteen feet away.

Erik's heart sank. Fighting his instinct to flee, he kept still, Toni crouched beside him. If he ran, he would be heard and most certainly would be shot.

But Bleddyn hadn't seen either of them. He stomped over to the shed and threw open the door. He leaned his gun against the outside wall, stepped inside and shone the light along Gary's hoard of cans.

Erik nudged Toni. "Stay here!" He crept out, seized the gun and retreated behind the back of the lean-to where the others were hiding. They could see into part of the shed through its open door.

Bleddyn aimed the beam along the lower shelves until he found a metal can, the old cylindrical type with a large screw-on lid and a spout, with the word *GAS* painted on the side. After placing his cigarette on the top shelf and the flashlight on the ground, he unscrewed the can's lid and sniffed the contents. He replaced the cigarette in his mouth, picked up the light, and started back to the lean-to, clasping the can against his chest with his left hand.

"DROP IT!" roared Erik, almost beside himself with anger. "Or I'll shoot your legs off!"

Toni jumped out of the bushes and aimed the beam directly into Bleddyn's eyes. Temporarily blinded, he stepped back, twisting his ankle on the uneven ground. He fell, dropping his flashlight while trying to hold on to the can. As it tipped against him, gas spilled down his clothes and flowed onto the ground beneath him.

The burning cigarette tumbled out of his mouth and landed on his trousers. With a whoosh, his pants exploded into yellow flames, ghastly shadows flickering against his distorted face. Screaming, he covered his eyes with his left arm and leapt to his feet, beating his clothes with his other hand as he ran blindly toward the sea. In the beam from Bronya's flashlight they watched Bleddyn fall down the bank and disappear from view.

"The shed!" yelled Toni. "The house will go up!"

A narrow band of flame shot along the ground toward the lean-to.

"The oil!" Erik warned.

"Water!" screamed Bronya, shining the beam onto the rain barrel at the corner of the lean-to. "Over there!" She ran toward it, followed by Toni, Mike and Dave, who tripped over Mike's heel almost knocking him down. Bronya threw the flashlight to the ground, yelling, "Push!" As they tipped the barrel over, water swamped the blaze, scattering the gas and extinguishing it before it could reach the lean-to.

Toni started for the dock. "I'm going to check on Gary," she yelled to Dave and Bronya who were already heading down the bank to see where Bleddyn had gone.

Erik handed the gun to Mike. "Here. You know about guns."

He checked it over quickly under the light of the lean-to and removed two shotgun shells, placing them in his pocket. "Wait, you guys!" he shouted. "We're coming with you." Turning to Erik he added, "I don't trust him an inch."

Erik reached Bronya first. "Not bad for someone who freaks out over fires!" he told her quietly. "That water barrel saved the house."

"No time to think," she explained.

They found the wet, burned man lying just above the water's edge, hand on his chest, moaning and gasping for breath. His hair, eyebrows and beard were singed, and parts of his trousers had melted onto his legs. When Erik smelled the distinctive odor of stale gas he knew why the explosion hadn't been more violent.

Bleddyn's wild eyes stared at him. "Can't breathe…"

"Get up," Erik said coldly, shining the flashlight on him.

"Can't…My heart…," mumbled Bleddyn.

Erik wondered if the drops on his face were sweat or water, but he wasn't about to get close enough to find out. "The hospital's a long way from here," he said, adding, "Isn't it a shame you sank the boat?" Seeing no reaction, Erik decided the man was telling them the truth about his heart.

"What are we going to do with him?" asked Bronya.

"Hospital," Erik said. "Except he can't walk."

"Gary's buggy, by the back door," suggested Dave. "I'll get it."

"I'll come too and shut up the house," Bronya said.

"Bring a couple of blankets and a tarp for Bleddyn," Erik called after them.

Bronya held the flashlight while Dave and Erik carefully rolled Bleddyn, still moaning, onto the sheet that Bronya had placed on top of the blankets. Dave caught sight of some burned paper sticking out of his back pocket. Deftly, he grabbed it and stuck it in his own jacket pocket before helping to maneuver Bleddyn into the almost too-small buggy, which already had the bundled tarp in it. "Hopkins Landing?" Dave asked as he helped pull the heavy wagon.

"It's the easiest place for an ambulance to get to," suggested Erik. "Yes," he told the sick man, "we're taking you to hospital."

Bronya followed. "Which boat?" she asked.

Mike thought a moment. "*Terpsichore?*"

Toni came up the ramp to meet them. "Gary's sounding a bit better, but we've still got to hurry."

"We're doing our best," Mike told her.

"I don't trust him being in the same boat as us," said Bronya, nodding her head in Bleddyn's direction. "It sure won't make Gary feel safe."

"We could put him in Al's boat and tow him," suggested Dave. "Bundle him up for warmth."

Everyone agreed that was the best solution.

"As soon as Erik gets *Terpsichore* started," said Toni, "Dave and I'll go ahead in one of the outboards and phone for the ambulance and the cops."

"Take *DC-3*," Erik told her. "There's a phone at the head of Gambier Harbor wharf."

They stopped where the hinged ramp descended steeply from the end of the dock. "Now what?" asked Dave.

Bronya moved to the front of the cart. "C'mon Dave. We'll go backward. Erik and Mike, hold the handle."

On the float at last, they lifted the swearing moaning man into

Al's boat, wrapped the blanket around him and covered him with the folded tarp.

Before attempting to start *Terpsichore*, Erik checked Gary's pulse as Toni had done. Ten heartbeats for ten seconds. Not so bad.

"Sure I'm alive?" murmured Gary.

"If you're dead," said Erik, "we're all dead." When he'd told Gary of their plans, the old man raised his thumb approvingly.

He must trust me, Erik said to himself as he removed the engine cover. I hope I can remember what he showed us. As he talked himself through the ignition procedure, the others waited in silence. Normally they would have laughed at Erik's behavior, but now they knew that the slightest distraction might cause a delay. Toni held the flashlight over the engine as Erik filled the little cups on the pistons with gas. "Turn the flywheel carefully until we hear the slurping sound," he said. Everyone held their breath and listened as the pistons inhaled the life-giving gas into the cylinder, waiting for the spark and resulting explosion. "Let 'er have it!" he yelled, spinning the flywheel vigorously before letting it go. With a cough and a distinctive *ka-putt, ka-putt, ka-putt*, *Terpsichore* cooperated. Everybody cheered.

Dave and Toni left for Gambier wharf in *DC-3*. As Erik passed Gary on the way to the wheel, the Welshman beckoned for him to come close.

"Good work," he told Erik. "Now make her waltz. Nice and easy, slow and smooth."

Moments later, the old boat was underway, towing Al's outboard and *Bailout* behind. Erik had never felt so frustrated. He'd always made fun of *Terpsichore*'s snail-like pace. And now, just when he wanted speed, it seemed to be going slower than usual. But he knew that it could be dangerous—perhaps even fatal—to subject Gary to the pounding ride of a small, planing boat like *Bailout*. He kept telling himself that *Terpsichore*'s displacement hull would provide the calmest ride. Nice and easy, slow and smooth, Gary had said.

Bronya tapped him on the back. "Gary says you're hired."

"Hey, Mike, would you take over for a bit?" Erik asked. He pointed to the glow reflected in the low clouds above the Langdale ferry slip. "Aim slightly to the left of that light."

"What happened?" Gary asked. "Bronya won't tell me."

Erik knelt down beside him. "It's okay, Gary. Everything's under control."

"Please," said Gary, "tell me."

Bronya pulled a couple of extra cushions off the seats and made him more comfortable. "Would you like some water?" she asked.

"Tea would be better," he mumbled.

While the tea was steeping, Gary said, a little more assertively, "Well, I'm waiting."

The three friends looked at each other, and Bronya began to tell him what had happened. When she reached the point where Bleddyn had locked them in the basement, she stopped to give Gary his tea, and Erik took over.

The old man didn't speak until they'd finished. "I can't take this in," he said at last. "Doesn't make sense. Tell me again tomorrow."

Ten minutes later Toni and Dave were back alongside, tying *DC-3* to the cleat.

"How's your head?" Toni asked Gary, her voice low.

"Tea's helping. Thanks," he grunted.

Bronya squeezed his hand. "It's okay. We understand."

Dave took off his floater jacket and hung it near the door. "The ambulance will be at Hopkins in thirty or forty minutes," he said. "Cops too."

Erik took over the wheel from Mike. "I guess no one thought to phone a parent?"

"Of course I did," Toni reassured him, "and he wasn't happy."

"Didn't you tell him what happened?" asked Bronya.

"Not exactly. It would only have worried them."

"Was it your dad?" asked Erik.

"No, yours."

Erik rolled his eyes.

WHEN THEY ARRIVED at Hopkins Landing, an ambulance and the police were waiting. After they had off-loaded Gary and Bleddyn and explained things to the police, Erik and his friends took *Terpsichore* and the other boats on to Gibsons. The police met them at the government dock and drove the five teenagers up to the police station to make their statements—but not before Erik had ordered enough Chinese take-out for all of them from a nearby restaurant. As they waited in the station, he pointed to the latest edition of the local paper that lay on the officer's desk. The headline read, "Summer Cabin Break-Ins on Gambier Island."

THE FOLLOWING DAY, Christmas, around lunchtime Erik picked up Toni to go and visit Gary at the hospital in Sechelt.

"Mom's up there," she told Erik as they drove onto the highway. "She got called in. One of the regular nurses is sick."

"Did you tell her to look out for Gary?"

"She phoned an hour ago and said he's doing fine. Nothing broken. And Bleddyn's been sent to Vancouver General."

"Good."

ERIK POINTED TO one of the ornaments on the large Christmas tree that greeted them in the foyer. "There's one of Dave's schlocky angels," he said. "We never did get them for Gary."

"That's okay," said Toni. "I've brought him something from our tree."

Gary was propped up in bed with a bandage around his head. A dish of three mince tarts sat on his bedside table.

"Happy Christmas!" they chorused.

Gary winced. "Yes it is, thanks to you," he said in a low voice.

"Sorry," Toni apologized. "I guess we ought to speak quietly."

"You sure sound a lot better than yesterday," said Erik. "How many stitches?"

"About eight," he grunted. "Mince tart?"

Erik declined. "Don't like raisins."

Toni helped herself. She looked at the other bed in the room. It was being used, but its occupant was somewhere else. "Not so good spending Christmas in here, huh?" she said.

Gary tried to nod, but stopped himself. "It sure beats lying in Davy Jones' locker any time of the year."

"Davy Jones' locker?" echoed Erik.

"Bottom of the sea—where the drowned sailors go…Now, I want to know exactly what went on up at my house last night."

They told him for the second time. "But what happened with you and Bleddyn in the boat?" Erik asked.

"When the others get here," he said. "Then I won't have to tell it twice."

At that moment he sound of squeaking running shoes and a chorus of loud voices came from down the corridor.

"Loudmouth Dave," muttered Toni. She walked over to the doorway as they approached and held her finger up to her mouth. "Sshh, you guys. Shut up!" she warned. "Gary's head's still hurting."

Dave, Mike and Bronya crept into Gary's room. They all exchanged greetings.

"I want to thank you people for the best Christmas present ever," Gary said.

"It's nothing," dismissed Mike.

"Don't give me that," Gary argued. "If you hadn't used your wits against that gun-toting drunk, I'd be dead."

"Cops been?" Mike asked.

"Yes."

"Where's Bleddyn?"

"They took him to Vancouver General yesterday on the last ferry," answered Gary, "in an ambulance. Under police guard."

Dave pulled the thick wad of partly burned damp paper out of his pocket and handed it to him. "I forgot to give you this yesterday. It was in Bleddyn's back trouser pocket."

"Dave!" said Bronya, aghast. "You should've given it to the police."

"There was too much going on. Anyway, I'll bet he stole it from Gary's house."

Toni and Dave peeled the bits apart and spread them over the bed. "Looks like a part of a legal form," said Bronya.

Gary squinted as he held up a bit of the printed paper. "Can't read without my glasses."

Dave grabbed a pair lying on the next locker. "Here, try these," he said, handing them over.

They worked well enough that Gary could recognize a few key words. "It's my will. And the remains of a new one that he brought. He must've stolen mine from the house so he could forge my signature."

"But what happened in the boat?" asked Mike.

"He wanted me to sign a will which he'd written, saying I'd left the farm to him. I refused. I gave him some whisky to make him forget what he'd come for. But it didn't work. I've always told myself that he couldn't be that bad. After all, he's my cousin."

"Perhaps he's changed," suggested Dave.

"Either that or I never knew him."

"But why did he wait so long before coming for what he thinks is his land?" asked Toni.

"The property wasn't worth much until prices began to climb. By then he was in prison."

"Why do you think he kept moving from place to place, living off the land?" asked Erik.

"Guess he was paranoid. After all, he was in prison a long time. And I'm sure he was hiding from me."

"Did he have a heart attack when he got burned?" Bronya asked.

Gary nodded. "A minor one, they said."

"No worse than he deserved," growled Dave.

Mike frowned. "He tried to murder you and burn the house down with three of us in it," he said indignantly. "He should spend the rest of his life in jail."

Toni took a Christmas tree ornament out of her backpack and placed it on Gary's bed. "When are they letting you out, Gary?" she asked.

"Couple of days. Who knows? X-ray's okay, blood tests are okay. They just want to make sure there's no bleeding inside the brain. What's this?" he asked, picking up a three-inch gold plastic figure dancing with a harp.

"This tree ornament's as close to *Terpsichore* as I could find. But I had to take her wings off because she wasn't an angel."

"Was she a bad girl?" asked Dave, trying to be funny.

Toni shook her head in mock disgust. "She's the spirit of dance."

"That's odd," said Erik. "She moves pretty slowly for a dancer."

Gary studied the figurine. "Slow and stately. But she brought me here, didn't she? Yep. She fits the bill. Thanks Toni. I'll glue this one onto the dash."

A nurse entered with a tray.

"Your second turkey dinner's here," Toni said.

They prepared to leave. "Guess we'd better let you eat in peace," said Erik.

"Yes, before your long-suffering parents blame me for making you late again," Gary said. "But there is something you people can do for me…If I'm not out of here within a couple of days, I'd appreciate it if you could check on the house. Don't want the pipes to freeze. Tell the cops first, though."

Erik nodded. "The generator will need topping up. Don't want the freezer to quit either. I'll go there tomorrow."

Dave pointed to the bits of paper spread over the bed. "What are you going to do with that mess?"

Gary began to pick the pieces up. "The police will want it as evidence," he answered. "I don't need it now. I was going to write another one anyway."

When they left Gary's room, Toni started them singing, "We wish you a Merry Christmas." As they walked down the corridor they didn't hear Gary's perfectly tuned, Welsh miner's voice sing quietly, "And a Happy New Year."

photo credit: Ryan Hanson

This is **Jo Hammond**'s first novel. A log salvor and longtime Sunshine Coast resident, Jo has found material for this exciting adventure story in her own experiences and those of her son.